COLLECTION MANAGEMENT

DAUGHTERS *of the* SEA

May

KATHRYN LASKY

DAUGHTERS of the SEA

May

SCHOLASTIC PRESS / NEW YORK

All rights reserved. Published by Scholastic Press, an imprint
of Scholastic Inc., *Publishers since 1920*. SCHOLASTIC, SCHOLASTIC PRESS, and
associated logos are trademarks and/or registered
trademarks of Scholastic Inc.

Library of Congress Cataloging-in-Publication Data

Lasky, Kathryn.
May / Kathryn Lasky.
p. cm.—(Daughters of the sea)
Summary: In 1899 on an island off the coast of Maine, fifteen-year-old
May learns why she has always felt different from the other girls in
her small town, but must keep hidden that she is a mermaid or risk
attracting the attention of a dangerous hunter, and losing a boy
for whom she cares
ISBN-13: 978-0-439-78311-8
ISBN-10: 0-439-78311-9
[1. Mermaids—Fiction. 2. Identity—Fiction. 3. Islands—Fiction.
4. Lighthouses—Fiction. 5. Maine—History—19th century—Fiction.]
I. Title.
PZ7.L3274May 2011
[Fic—dc22
2010026535

<Fantasy>
YA Fic.

Printed in the U.S.A.   23
First edition, March 2011

The text type was set in ITC Cheltenham Book.
Book design by Lillie Howard

Exultation is the going
Of an inland soul to sea,
Past the houses — past the headlands —
Into deep Eternity —

Bred as we, among the mountains,
Can the sailor understand
The divine intoxication
Of the first league out from land?

—Emily Dickinson

PROLOGUE

MAINE COAST, OFF
SIMON'S LEDGE, 1883

THE FOG HAD SET IN THICK after the storm, pushed by a southeast wind. But he couldn't wait any longer. He had to check his traps. When the nor'easter had blasted through two days before, it had been fierce— almost hurricane force, although it wasn't the season. A ship had gone down, and two fishing trawlers were lost to the south, somewhere off Georges Bank. No hope for any of those vessels. He would keep his eye out for debris. He was worried about his lobster traps—how many had broken free from their buoys or been dragged by the turmoil of confused winds and currents that followed a storm of such force? If a fisherman was out now it wasn't the storm itself that was threatening but the aftermath. It was the lost gear, the lost lobsters, the lost money.

His income tending the Egg Rock Lighthouse was barely adequate. But between lobstering and getting the occasional deck job on a trawler he could make just about enough for their life at the lighthouse. He and his wife had never been blessed with children. It would be hard, he supposed, to support a child—not with all the doctoring that Zeeba required. She had just gone to a new doctor last month over in Surrey, who had given her some different stomach powders. They cost, they did! He wondered if a baby would have made a difference for them, for their marriage.

But her numerous afflictions required Zeeba's full attention; she kept meticulous charts recording her fevers, bodily functions, and pulse rate. Hepzibah Plum always set off for the doctor well armed, dauntingly armed, with information. One doctor even told her that she could be a doctor. That was probably the happiest day of Zeeba's life. She came back to Egg Rock absolutely hooting about that.

Edgar Plum peered into the fog. So dense. If it

would only begin to fray a bit, unravel the gray so that he could see something—even just the loom, or the dark shadow of the island that lifted out of the fog. He was looking for Burnt Porcupine, where he had set some traps. He caught the fishy smell of seals basking in the thick mists of fog on the ledge, so he must be near.

The chop diminished, and the water now was relatively calm. Everything seemed unusually quiet. No sound of waves slapping into one another. The remaining noises were intermittent and yet distinct— the luff of his sail as it relaxed in this windless pocket of air, the distant disembodied chimes of a bell buoy cut by the whine of a seagull's cry. All these were familiar to him. But then something caught his attention. It was an odd noise—wood? Possibly. A timber or maybe a lobster trap come loose, drifting about, smacked by something. But suddenly there was another sound, a tone that laced through the fog. He froze at the tiller of his small sailing skiff. It was a sweet babbling sound, so sweet, so merry— so human?

He quickly lowered his sail, put out his oars, and began rowing toward the soft, cozy babbling. As he drew nearer he saw a shape in the water. It was rectangular—a sea chest. The lid was flopped open and only attached with one hinge. On either side a dolphin swam, gently poking it this way or that when it listed too far to one side or the other. Overhead a seagull hovered. Edgar Plum caught his breath as he spied a tiny hand waving in the air.

A baby! He was almost too frightened to row toward it, but the dolphins, as if sensing his presence, began to steer the sea chest toward him. The fog had blown off, and rags of mist hung in the air as he looked down and saw the sweet face of an infant with red curls like a luminous cloud of dawn light.

When he picked up the infant he saw that it was wrapped as snug as could be in a gray knit blanket covered by an oilskin cloak. The baby was a girl, as he had suspected when he first saw her. He made a sling so he could carry her neatly under his sou'wester jacket. Before he raised his sail, he reached over and fetched the chest and its lid from the water. When he brought it over the gunwales he could see letters carved on the lid's top—HMS *Resolute.*

"HMS *Resolute!* My word!" Edgar Plum whispered to himself. That was the ship that had gone down off Georges Bank. He stared into the wind that had just sprung up now from the northwest. It had reversed, for the wind had been blowing for the last two days out of the southeast—*driving this baby right to me,* he thought. He was so brimful of joy that he nearly whooped out loud. It was meant to be. The report said everyone was lost. No hope. But this was hope. *We'll call her Hope,* he thought.

❀   ❀   ❀

They would not call her Hope. When Edgar got home with his bundle, Hepzibah Plum was hanging her head over a pot of steaming camphor broth to treat her lungs.

"Zeeba! Zeeba! Come out from under that tent of yours. I got a surprise for you."

"Hold your horses." Her voice floated out from the toweling that covered her head and trapped the vapor. "Just another minute."

But it was only another few seconds before the baby cried out. Zeeba tore the toweling off her head. Her face was red and blotchy. "What's that?" She had a thin, angular face, and her cheekbones protruded so that they cast shadows into the hollows beneath them. Around her mouth were vertical crinkles as if invisible drawstrings needed to be pulled for any utterance.

"What in the name of Jesus have you brought home, Gar?"

"A baby, Zeeb, a baby for us."

"Us?"

"Come on now, come look at her. She's pretty as can be."

Hepzibah Plum took mincing steps toward her husband. The drawstrings had pulled taut again, and the hole of her mouth had closed tight. Gar looked at her, expecting an "ooh" or an "aah" of astonishment and wonder. But no sound was emitted. In fact, her lips pressed tighter together.

You won't need no more medicines. No more powders, Gar thought. "God has finally blessed us with a child." A dark look seeped from Zeeba's eyes, but Edgar was oblivious. "We'll call her Hope."

Zeeba's brow contracted in a frown. The vertical lines between her eyebrows deepened. "No! We'll call her Mabel."

"Mabel?" Edgar said weakly.

"Yes; Mabel, after my mother. How'd you come by her?"

But Gar knew it was not because Zeeba was honoring her mother. She wanted people to think that she, Hepzibah Plum, was not barren but had at last given birth. She was putting her mark on the child. It was in that moment that Gar decided that he would never tell his wife the truth about where he had found this baby.

"I was down near Crockett Cove." He decided he had to make it as far away as possible. "A woman down there died in childbirth; no relatives, nothing."

Hepzibah sighed. "Probably a bastard child."

The word went through Edgar like an electrical current. "She ain't no bastard, Hepzibah. Don't you ever call her that! She's ours, and we'll treat her that way, like she was born to us. You and me." He took a deep breath. "And we'll call her May for short." Hepzibah blinked at her husband. She had never heard him speak in this low, firm voice before. It almost scared her. "We got to feed her now. She's hungry. We got any milk?"

"If you go out and milk Bells we do."

He started to hand the baby to his wife. She backed away. "I got to go milk the cow, Zeeba, you just said so."

"I'll do it. You hold the baby."

This was the first time in their ten years of married life that Hepzibah Plum had ever milked their cow. As she walked out the door of the lighthouse she turned and said, "You know, I thought I was getting a mite better in my camphor tent there." She nodded toward the pot simmering on the stove. "But this interruption hasn't helped."

"She's not an interruption, Zeeb, she's our daughter. She's May Plum."

Zeeba pressed her colorless lips into a firm line and turned to the door.

WINTER 1898

THE BROKEN CHIMNEY

IT WAS A LATE-SEASON NOR'EASTER. The wind screeched round the squat frame house, and the clapboards moaned periodically as if in reply. Every now and then the light tower that thrust upward sixty-four feet into the storm-rent sky seemed to sway just a bit. But it had been there for decades and had not yet been felled by any weather. May Plum sat in a pool of lamplight, darning a sock. Her mother, across the kitchen in her rocker, had put a compress over her eyes.

"You know, if my eyes hadn't got so poor I'd be helping you with them socks. I got to go to that new doctor that's come to the village as soon as this weather breaks."

"It ain't going to break for the next few days, Zeeb," Gar called from his chair. "This wind done set in. It's blowin' like . . ." May kept her eyes on the sock. She could feel her mother tense without looking at her. She knew what was coming, but her father caught himself just in time and swerved mid sentence to avoid cursing. "Blowin' like stink," he concluded. May knew what would happen next. She knew them, this room, this island all too well. Nothing ever really changed. She could predict every sigh and groan of her mother, every word her father might or might not speak, depending on how much he had drunk. She heard his sleeve brush the table and she knew that it would be followed by the splash of whiskey being poured into the mug.

Nothing ever changed, not even the seasons. It might be late for nor'easters but in truth, May realized, there was just one season in the lighthouse—winter. It was always dark yet always too hot inside because of her mother's insistence on keeping the fire in the cast-iron cook-and-heat stove going. Spring might come, and while others flung open their windows and hung out their linens to catch the fresh breezes for a good airing out, Zeeba did not, for she was deeply suspicious of drafts. She regarded these diabolical streams of air as a kind of roaming executioner that could strike anytime. She was always on the alert for an insinuating breeze that in her mind was as pestilent as a rat-borne plague, as infectious as a flea-ridden rabid dog.

Come summer, if the wind was in the right direction, May could catch the joyous shrieks and whoops of children swimming off the town wharf. But she was forbidden from entering the water. When she went to town with her father on a hot day it was almost painful for her to watch the swimmers. Their hair plastered to their heads made them seem sleek as seals and more beautiful than they actually were. It was mostly boys who swam, not girls. Perhaps the wet clothing revealed too much of what was beneath the light cottons and muslins that clung to the girls' bodies. May's own figure had begun to change in the last year. She was particularly conscious of Zeeba's furtive glances and odd comments referring to her robust health while staring at her waist or the bodice of her dress, which might be a bit tight. But still, it was all she could do not to jump in when she heard those children squealing with delight as they ran off the wharf into the water.

And when they reemerged she gaped at them in wonder, for their skin glistened with saltwater. She craved the feeling of those rivulets of seawater that coursed down their arms. She saw the sparkling little liquid spheres caught in their eyelashes and wondered what it felt like to look through a scrim of water drops. Like glistening travelers from far away, the children climbed from the harbor onto the wharf, carrying their souvenirs from another world. The streamlets of water that traced patterns on their shoulders, the twinkling drops in their eyelashes, the rime of salt that formed on their skin as the children baked themselves dry in the sun—these were their keepsakes, their mementos, their artifacts from that lovely and mysterious underwater world.

But could May join them? Never. Swimming was the one subject on which her father and mother agreed. Zeeba objected because "normal" girls didn't swim. But a few did. May had seen them jumping off the dock in their petticoats. There was no use arguing with her parents, however.

Her father seemed genuinely fearful of her swimming. "Your mother's right, de-ah. Swimming never brought anybody any good. Bad for your lungs. My uncle, he went overboard. Was only in the water for a minute, no more, and was never the same again." Gar would not permit her to even wade on the beach of the calm inlet on the back side of Egg Rock Island where the sea furrowed in.

May stole a glance up from her mending and regarded her parents. They both sat in thick shadows. Until they could get to the mainland for oil, the Plums could only use one lamp in the kitchen. It was against the regulations of the lighthouse service board to use its high-quality kerosene for domestic purposes. They were running low on ordinary lamp oil, and since May was doing the darning she got the light. But she did have schoolbooks she wanted to read. Those had to be read in daylight only. "Can't waste light on books!" That was Zeeba's constant refrain. The only book that light was wasted on was the Bible. That was the single exception.

School had been May's only escape from the lighthouse and the unceasing narrative of Zeeba's illnesses. But before the storm set in her mother had had a bad spell with her stomach and insisted that May stay home from school in Bar Harbor, on the big island of Mount Desert, for most of the past month. Then just when her mother was feeling better the storm hit so it was impossible for her father to take her in the skiff, even though it was a short sail. She would be behind in everything! And whenever she did open her books, Zeeba seemed to resent it. It wasn't simply what she said that suggested her irritation with "book learning," as Zeeba called it, but her dark glances, the little snorts that issued forth every time May sat down to read or try to do arithmetic problems in the math book. She had a peculiar way of staring at her, staring at May so hard it felt as if Zeeba's eyes were drilling through her. And they did. They wrecked her concentration. She couldn't believe how many mistakes she had made in a simple set of fractions. It was useless to be in the same room with her mother when she was trying to do homework.

But May couldn't wait to get back to school even if she was behind in every subject. If only Zeeba wouldn't get sick again! She glanced at her mother and then at the lamp.

Meanwhile, the storm continued to rage outside, sealing them off more completely than ever from the big island of Mount Desert. The mail boat had not come out for days now. Too rough. Not that May ever received a letter. Still, it was nice to go down to the pier when Captain Weed delivered her parents' mail.

The stifling predictability of her life in this house, on this drear and forlorn rockbound tiny island in a boiling sea, was almost too much. Why had it begun to grate on her so intensely these last few months? She had lived with it all her life, but right now she felt as if she could not stand another minute. The space was too tight. There was really only room for Zeeba and her sicknesses.

In general Hepzibah Plum preferred the word *fail* to *sick*. Her eyes were failing, her lungs were failing, her arthritic joints were failing, and, of course, her heart, with its strange syncopated rhythms, was failing. But even preferable to the word *fail* was *complications*. *Complications* suggested the awesome mystery of her illnesses. She was extremely proud of her heart, with its peculiar beat. It had defied diagnosis by all the best doctors from Bar Harbor to Eastport and right on down south and west to Cape Rosier. It was Hepzibah's dream to go to Boston and be examined by the finest doctors in America at the Massachusetts General Hospital. She lived to be diagnosed with something horrific, and then presumably die very happily. *Happily ever after* had a meaning for Hepzibah that had nothing to do with storybooks or fairy tales. It meant a death dignified and certified by Boston doctors.

May looked again at Zeeba. How could she be so different from her own mother? Her mother's hair, thin and dark with iron-gray streaks, was skinned straight up into a knob that perched on top of her head. It was pulled so tight that it seemed to May to have permanently dragged the top of Hepzibah's ears into two sharp points, as if they were trying to leap up there and keep company with that nodule of hair. Her face appeared waxen and was grooved rather than wrinkled. Two deep trenches ran from either side of her nose to the corners of her thin, colorless lips. There were liver spots on her cheekbones, and beneath her eyes there were small gray pouches with a tinge of yellow that reminded May of raw clams.

It was not simply that May and Hepzibah were as unlike in appearance as any mother and daughter could be, but they were just as different on the inside as well. None of May's organs were failing. She had hardly been sick a day in her life. She was robust and brimming with health, a health that her mother seemed to almost resent. The closest she ever came to voicing any bitterness was when she would regard May while she was hoeing in the garden or lugging an immense basket of wet laundry to hang out to dry. On those occasions Zeeba would sigh deeply, shake her head, and say wearily, "I do envy that girl's strength." Then in a slightly lower voice she might whisper, "Almost unnatural, though," and look at May as if she were a complete stranger.

And although May did not envy her mother's ill health she sometimes wondered if her mother would like her more if she were weaker, more fragile. Would it please her mother to see her very, very sick? Would it bring out a tenderness in her? May thought about the mothers and daughters in Bar Harbor walking arm in arm down the street, window-shopping or maybe even in summer buying an ice cream to share. Those mothers and daughters seemed as if they belonged together whether they looked alike or not. They were coupled through deep feelings. Did those girls ever catch their mothers looking at them as if they were complete strangers? Did they feel out of place in their own families, as if they didn't quite belong?

"Belong." She whispered the word to herself and felt a deep and terrible overwhelming sadness flood through her. The wind temporarily eased and then a few seconds later began again with a thin wail that built to a mournful lament as it scoured around the corners of the house and pried shingles from the roof.

May turned her gaze to look out the window at the two five-second flashes as they swept across the snow. These two flashes were followed by a ten-second gap. This was the "signature" of the Egg Rock Light, or its characteristic sequence. Each lighthouse along the coast of the country had its own sequence designed to aid mariners in distinguishing one light from another. The flashes were like parentheses in the darkness of the long winter nights whose shadows clung like lint through the short day when hours of light were whittled away minute by minute.

May and her father maintained their light. It was a great deal of work. In all there were over one hundred and fifty instructions for proper lighthouse keeping. The first was that the lamps must be lit at sunset and kept continually burning "bright and clear" until sunrise. It was the extraordinary lens that multiplied the light of the kerosene lamp through its array of prisms, bending it into horizontal sprays. It was a beacon for ships at sea, warning them of The Bones, rock ledges that lurked just beneath the surface and earned their name from the lives they had claimed from innumerable shipwrecks before Egg Rock Light had been built. Edgar Plum's father had been the first lighthouse keeper of the rock. And now Edgar had tended it for thirty years. When the weather was foggy or stormy, the light was kept burning both day and night.

May put down her darning and went to the window to watch the sweep of the light more closely.

"You see it, don't you, de-ah?" her father said.

"Yes, Pa, I think that wick is smoking again."

"Well, time to wind anyhow. I'll tend to it." From the watch room they could service the light, wind the clockworks, oil its gears, and then climb up a short ladder to get inside the lens itself, which rose like an immense glass beehive. Once inside they could stand on the slowly rotating platform and trim the wick of the lamp.

May looked at the bottle on the table. It was almost empty. But she would not say anything. She never did. No matter how much her father drank he was never too unsteady to climb the winding stairs of the sixty-four-foot tower to the watch room, just below the lantern room. But he seemed tired tonight. "I'll go up, Pa. I need to stretch my legs."

"So do I," he laughed, and rose to start the climb.

"You know, I swear I can smell those fumes down here," Zeeba moaned. "The durned thing ain't vented properly. I think that's what's been giving me a head-ache. And of course that's no help for my eyes. Or maybe that's what gets to my eyes first and why they be failing and then that gives me the headache. Vicious circle, it is."

"Oh, Mother, I don't think the fumes could come down here," May said. "You know they rise with the heat up in the lantern room."

"It's back-drafting. Don't contradict me, child. You think you know so much. Well, you don't."

May listened. She had a keen ear for all noises. The cries of the cormorants when they spotted a school of mackerel; the flap of a schooner's sails buried in the howling wind as it tacked across the bay. And she knew the sound when the lantern was not vented properly, and this lantern was not back-drafting.

Since as long as she could remember, May had helped her father with the light, simple tasks at first like hanging the brushes up neatly after he had dusted off the prisms. She liked these lighthouse-tending chores. They were so different from the odious tasks involved in tending her mother—emptying her bed-pan when she was too tired to do her business in the privy, mixing up the endless potions, preparing hot or sometimes cold compresses depending on which body part was "failing."

It was not very long until May was able to help her father trim the wick, wind up the clockworks, and her favorite—polish the lens with the brushes and the special solutions. She loved climbing into the glass beehive and slowly turning around, caught in the glittering reflections of the prisms. The prisms intrigued her. It seemed magical to her how they multiplied and focused light.

So she asked Miss Lowe, who was the librarian in Bar Harbor. Miss Lowe was eager to answer her questions and very excited. She took out what looked like a triangular piece of glass from her drawer. "Come over to the window," she said. She held it up to the light, and suddenly what had been a simple beam of sunlight on one side of the prism became bent bands of colored light.

"It's like a rainbow!" May exclaimed.

Miss Lowe found as many books as she could with information about prisms. Rainbows, May learned, were nothing more than millions upon millions of water droplets through which the sun's rays passed and bent and split into bows of color. She thought of those droplets she had seen ensnared in the eyes of the children who dove off the wharf.

For her birthday that year Miss Lowe had given

May a small prism of her own, which she hung up in her room and watched as the light passed through on sunny days, casting shimmering spots of color onto her bare walls.

May now heard her father's footsteps receding as he climbed higher in the tower. She was about to pick up another sock and begin darning when there was a horrendous crash, then a stuttering of light across the snowfields.

"The lantern!" May screeched, jumping out of her chair. She raced up the winding stairs. There were always buckets of water up there in case of fire, but she did not smell kerosene or smoke. However, she did hear a ragged groan and then a gasp.

"Pa! Pa! Oh my God!" she yelped. Her father was on the rotating platform of the lens. There was blood on his hand, but no fire, and the lens was still rotating in its housing. But something had shattered. Then she saw the shards of the lantern's chimney. As if to confirm this the light was stammering into the night! The signature of the flash would be broken, the characteristic sequence of the Egg Rock Light garbled, and sailors would become confused and their vessels fetch up on the deadly rocks and ledges.

May was stunned. She felt herself at the vortex of a frightening collision of events. Her father was bleeding, the chimney was broken, and the night was growing wilder.

Then the unthinkable occurred.

"What the devil! That drunken old fool! I knew it! I knew it!"

Hepzibah Plum stood in the doorway of the watch room. She was a tower of dark, glowering rage. She glared at her husband. Her eyes settled on the star that was sewn on the lapel of the indigo blue coat, the uniform that all keepers were required to wear. The star was awarded to keepers who had been commended for efficiency four consecutive quarterly inspections by the lighthouse service board. "They're going to rip that star right from your jacket, Mr. Plum!"

"Mother!" was all May could say. Never in her entire life had May seen her mother in the tower. Never had she climbed the stairs. But never had her father fallen, and never had the chimney shattered and the signature of the light been scrambled.

Suddenly May felt as if her entire world was as fragile as that glass chimney, and was breaking all around her, threatening to crush her at any moment.

THE SURGE WITHIN

HER FATHER'S CUT WAS NOT AS BAD as the blood indicated. But Gar had injured his hip and was in great pain. It would be days before he could walk enough to get himself down the winding stairs. "Don't worry about me! Don't worry about me!" he kept repeating as May bandaged his hand. "I'll be okay. Look—the light's still working. You've stopped my bleeding. We're still a lighthouse." He gazed around the neat, spare lantern room with its small workbench, neatly arranged tools, and gleaming wood floors that May waxed twice a month.

"We got a spare chimney you can fetch," Gar said.

"But it's not as good, Pa, as the one that's broke."

"It'll do for now. We'll order a new one soon as we can."

Somehow May managed to get her father down from the circular platform to the service area. She ran back down the winding stairs to bring him blankets and pillows so he could rest more comfortably.

From the floor of the service area one could look straight up into the dome of the lantern room with its large glass storm panes and polished brass fixtures. The only decoration in the entire lantern room was a small figure of Saint Anthony, the patron saint against shipwrecks, attached to a narrow panel between two of the windows. Almost every lighthouse up and down the east coast of the United States had either a painting or a carved figure of this saint, who was also charged with a vaguer mission as the saint of "lost things."

She noticed the figure was slightly askew on its hook.

Her father patted her hand. "Now, don't you worry none, May. We'll get a replacement for the chimney soon as we can get ashore. I got a spare here like I said."

May knew this, but the spare did not draft as well; the wick in the lantern wouldn't burn as steadily. But her father kept trying to reassure her. "Ships can still see us, de-ah. We're still a lighthouse and I'm the keeper. With your help we'll do fine. Now, if you could fetch me a cup of tea, that would set well."

Hepzibah, who had remained in the service area, or watch room, had hardly said a word since her initial outburst but merely pressed her lips together, then turned around and began to descend the stairs, accompanied by a stentorian array of groans, inhalations, and exhalations that telegraphed her fury.

For Hepzibah Plum, that consummate miser of illness with her insatiable greed for suffering, it was unimaginable that she was not the only one whose body was now failing. Her avarice for illness became so overwhelming that she headed straight for her bed like a passenger embarking on a transoceanic passage who grew seasick if she ventured on deck.

In addition to keeping up with the usual lighthouse-tending chores, May became a full-time nurse for both her parents.

The first day after the accident May thought she herself might collapse from running between two patients separated by fifty-eight feet of vertical distance. Her mother became more demanding than ever. Illness was not something to be shared, divided. May was called to rub her mother's poor cramping feet; fetch the endless array of powders, pills, and tonics; cook special broths for her failing stomach, her bladder complications, her heart palpitations.

"Bring me my powders, May," Zeeba croaked from her bed.

May came in, stirring the glass with the greenish powders vigorously with a small spoon. "I'm doing it just like you like them. No bits left in the bottom."

"Good," Zeeba replied. May handed her the drink. While she sipped, Zeeba kept her eyes leveled on May, then handed the glass back. "You understand why you can't go back to school when the weather breaks."

May tried to hold the glass steady, but a rage boiled just beneath her skin.

"Well . . . I mean if Pa's okay and—"

Zeeba cut her off. "Pa will be fine. But I'm declining, and I need you here. Pa can't fix my medicines, and soon as this storm clears out it will be allergy season. It's always that way."

"But that's spring. That doesn't come until late April or so."

"Storms bring it on early."

"But, Mother—"

"Don't 'but, Mother' me!" Hepzibah snapped, and sank back on her pillows.

If she had felt stifled before, May was almost suffocating now. She was cut off more with each passing minute. There was no respite, no chance to escape. It was as if a noose were tightening and she was being strangled, gasping.

She began to imagine the interminable dreariness in which she was destined to grow old. She pictured an old withered version of herself—her red hair fading to gray, wrinkles scoring her face, her generous lips becoming thin and pale, clamped tight trying to hide purple toothless gums as the years slipped by and she tended not one but two invalid parents. The future loomed ahead with a relentless grimness that was crushing.

On the second night after Gar's accident the wind gusts became so strong the lantern room in the tower actually began to sway. Beyond the rattling windows, May heard another sound.

This was not the shrieks of the wind nor the shrill cries of seagulls. This sound threaded through the crashing of waves on the rocks. It was that of a human voice crying out in the midst of the storm.

"Pa! There's someone out there!" she gasped.

"What?" He looked bewildered. How could she hear anything through the din of the storm?

"There is someone out there!" May was amazed herself but certain that she had heard a voice crying out.

"But—but—" her father stammered. "The light's been working."

"Pretty good, yes. But someone is out there, Pa. He's in trouble."

The light had been working as best it could. The backup chimney, it turned out, was slightly chipped, causing the light to waver just a fraction because of imperfect drafting. There was a stuttering hiss she had detected. Had that affected the beams of refracted light? She wasn't sure. But maybe, in that sliver left dark by the stuttering, a ship . . . She did not complete the thought but raced over to the telescope and pressed her eye to it, then turned the eyepiece to focus. She gasped in horror. Through the wind and crashing waves she saw it—the three spindly masts of a coastal schooner slanting into the night. They were leaning almost parallel to the sea, and the hull of the ship lay on its side like a mortally wounded creature. Immense waves crashed over the rock ledges, scouring the wreck.

"Pa, there's a ship on The Bones! It's on The Bones!" She pressed her eye so hard against the scope's eyepiece that she would have a half ring printed beneath it for almost a day. The sight through the lens was terrifying, and she began to relate what she saw to her father. She heard him trying to drag himself to a window, but his hip was so bad he couldn't stand. "Stay there," May ordered. "I'll tell you everything. They're launching a surfboat from the rescue station!"

A half dozen men were climbing into the craft to man the oars. It would be a race between the men in the surfboat and the fury of the sea. She saw the captain of the surfboat standing in the stern, trying to steer with a gigantic oar through the raging sea to the wrecked schooner on the ledges. It seemed to take forever.

"It must be Duncan captaining the surfboat," her father offered.

"Well, whoever it is, he's having a time of it getting close."

"'Course he would. Too close he'll get snagged in the rigging."

Periodically May would gasp and think all was lost as the surfboat disappeared into the deep trough of a wave and then in the next instant reappear and seem to hover ten feet above the wreck.

"The bow oarsman just heaved a big grappling hook with a line attached. I think he got it hooked on the stern rail. Almost! Almost!" May was nearly jumping up and down. But then a tremendous wave cracked the schooner in half, the masts plunged into the sea, and the ship was scrubbed off The Bones. She gasped as she saw three bodies falling into the water.

Two men stood up in the bow of the surfboat. A tiny spark of hope was kindled when she saw they stood with life rings to toss. Yes, there was a man in the water clinging to a piece of wood. They were close, but each time she felt they might grab him, a wave pushed them back. Finally, they flung a line that unfurled like scribbling in the darkness.

Just at that moment she spotted another man. He was not that far away, and yet she was not sure if the men on the surfboat saw him. May felt something rise up inside her. She turned from the telescope and ran down the stairs.

"Where are you going?" her father shouted. "May, where are you going? You can't do nothing. The surfboat is out there! Don't you go out there. Don't! Don't go near the water. May!"

But she was already out the door. She could hear the surfboat's men yelling to the sailors and the sailors' desperate cries lacing the night. She raced down to the dock and clung to a piling. Suddenly the snow and rain cleared and the moon staggered out from behind oily clouds, casting a ghastly light on a scene of wild destruction. She held on to the piling and leaned out as far as she could. She had no fear of this water. She had never been afraid of this sea. Why then was her father so fearful? She'd seen something deeper than any rational fear inscribed on his face when she ran from the house. It was terror—absolute terror.

Her eyes were now fastened on the man that the crew of the surfboat did not see. Every second she stood there watching the drowning man, she felt as if the surge of the sea were rising within her, empowering her. She tried to yell over the wind, but it slammed the words back down her throat. There was a man drowning seventy-five feet from where she stood on the pier, and yet the sailors in the surfboat did not see him. Once more she began screaming. Her throat was raw. Tears streamed from her eyes. She had to force herself not to let go of the piling and dive into the sea. She knew she could swim. She'd never done it, but she knew it just as she knew she could breathe. A startling thought seized her. *I can breathe water.*

It was unimaginable that she could stand by and watch a man drown. She knew water. Somewhere deep inside of her she knew the tides, the currents, the ways of water, the sea. But the memory of Gar's ashen face loomed in her mind, so May finally tore herself away and retreated to the lighthouse.

"May! May! You came back." Her father seemed surprised, with disbelief in his eyes. "You're all right?"

"Of course I'm all right. It's the fellows out there who aren't."

"The schooner's gone?"

"A wave got it; biggest wave I ever saw."

"Lucky they didn't get the heaving grapple hooked on it or they would have been drug right under." He looked at her hard now. "May, you were crazy to run out there like that! Just crazy." His chin seemed to quiver as he spoke, and his lower lip moved as if he wanted to say more.

What was it that he so feared about her going near the water? She lived on an island. They had to go back and forth all the time to the mainland in their own skiff. Her father's crushing anxiety made no sense. She looked away, avoiding the shadow of terror that lingered in his eyes.

SOUNDS WITHIN THE STORM

THE MEN FROM THE SURFBOAT had brought three of the rescued sailors of the *Josiah B. Harwood* into the lighthouse. A fourth's body had been recovered and lay on a cot, his rock-bashed head covered with a sheet. *Was that the one I could have saved?* May thought. She could not tear her eyes from the sheet. The anonymity of the lumpy form beneath it appalled her. But the bashed body marked with the violence of the sea might be even worse. She spotted fingertips peeking out from under the sheet. They were so normal looking, slender and long and with calluses from hard work. How could this little part of the dead man look so normal? What had that hand held aside from ropes and fishnets? Had it ever stroked a child's hair or held a woman's hand at a dance?

"The other fellow we couldn't reach." A voice interrupted her thoughts. "He'll most likely fetch up tomorrow on the south side of the island," said the skipper of the surfboat. He looked down and shook his head. "The rest went over on the far side of The Bones, and they most likely got dragged straight out to sea."

"Where's your pa?" A tall young man May recognized from the summer came up to her. He held his knitted watch cap in his hand in a gesture of gentlemanly politeness that seemed rather ludicrous given the situation.

"He's up in the tower. He fell tending the lantern—hurt his hip and can't manage stairs."

"And your ma?" the man asked.

"She's poorly." And perhaps a bit too quickly, May felt the need to assure the men in the room that they need not worry, even though she was quite unsure of herself. "But I can take care of things."

"My name's Rudd—Rudd Sawyer. I seen you last summer some. I fish—lobster—with Cap'n Haskell, here, when he's not fishing drowning folks out of the water."

"I'm May—May Plum."

"You have to take care of things here, I guess." He looked around. She had lit several kerosene lamps, and the light glanced off his dark curly brown hair, burnishing it to a deep bronze.

"I manage," she replied mechanically.

"Expect you do, but it's not going to be pretty or easy if you find that body all bloated up."

May looked down. Less than an hour ago, that "body" had been alive and could have been saved. "Let me get some more chowder for all of you." She walked back to the stove. She could feel his eyes following her.

She ladled out chowder, fetched some cheese from the cold larder, and was about to slice some bread, when he was by her side. "Here, I'll help you do that, May."

"I said I could manage," she said a bit too sharply. She was not used to people paying much attention to her, especially an attractive young man older than the boys she knew in school.

"I don't doubt it," he said with an undisguised twinkle in his eye.

Was this fellow actually flirting with her? There was a dead man on the cot, three others half drowned, and a body swirling out in the eddies off the island. Yet this Rudd Sawyer put his hand on top of hers, took the knife, and started cutting the loaf of bread. The touch of his hand sent a surprising thrill through her. She caught her breath, feeling a twinge of guilt, and pulled away.

"May!" It was her mother's voice from the back bedroom. "May, what's going on?"

"I told you, Ma," May called back. "Ship went up on The Bones. We got Captain Haskell here with his crew from the *Alba Jean*."

"Well, I need my stomach powders now! My digestion's in a frightful way and—"

"Yes, Ma!" May felt the color rise in her cheeks. She was mortified. How her mother could be talking about her stomach, her digestion, at a time like this defied all reason.

May looked over at Rudd. "She's—she's—"

"Poorly," Rudd said with a sympathetic half smile.

May was too embarrassed to say anything. She turned and went to fetch the powders her mother demanded.

When she had tended to her mother, she took chowder and bread up to her father and assured him that the broken chimney had not caused the catastrophe. Although in truth she could not be certain. Then she returned to the kitchen. Rudd had gone out to bring wood in from the shed to build up the fire in the stove and the hearth. "Wind seems to be dying down," he said when he came in with several logs.

"Hope so," Captain Haskell replied. "Question is if it dies down enough should we try and haul these fellows out of here?" He nodded at the rescued men, who were lying on the piles of bedding that May had fixed up for them. "Or bring the doctor here? That one in the corner looks like he might be working up to pneumonia. Lungs sound wheezier than a pecked set of bellows."

There indeed was an ominous rattle coming from the man's chest. Captain Haskell turned to May. "You should get on to sleep, May. You've done enough for the night. We can't thank you for all your kindnesses."

May glanced toward the cot, where the figure of the dead man peaked and dipped beneath the sheet like a forsaken landscape. "Don't worry none about him. We'll get him out of here first thing," the captain said.

She shook her head softly and began to say something, but words failed her. How could she explain that it was not just the drowned man who she was worried about but the lost sailor as well? The other she had seen so clearly when they had not, the other, whom she thought she could have saved. She felt Rudd Sawyer's eyes again resting on her. She touched her hair nervously. She was not accustomed to anyone looking at her—at least not in this way—and not a very handsome man.

"Well, good night," she said. And not even daring to look at him she went to her bedroom. She knew his eyes were following her.

But sleep seemed impossible. Her mind kept turning to her father and his completely irrational fear of her going into the water. Yes, she understood that he did not want her to jump into a stormy sea. That made sense. But that look of terror on his face had revealed more than just a momentary fear. Until she had turned fourteen she had never thought about it much before, but now that she was almost sixteen her urge to swim sometimes seemed overwhelming but never as intense as on this night. She had a mind to dash up those stairs and ask him. Demand that he give her an explanation. But how could she? Every time she thought of the terror she had seen in his eyes she knew she could not ask him. She couldn't bear to cause him any more pain.

She was haunted by the notion that one of the sailors had died tonight. And then there was the other man whose body was yet to be recovered. Where was he now? But more insistently another question haunted her: Why did she have this certainty that she could have saved both of them?

She listened to the storm, which had lessened somewhat. Having lived so close to the sea all her life, she knew intimately the sounds of wind and water in all of its moods. She could hear tiny noises that other people never heard. It was as if she could tease them out from the fabric of churning water. If she listened carefully she could hear beyond the roar of the storm and identify the rustlings of water as it swirled deeper beneath the crashing waves, the fizzing sound of the long curling combers that ran in over Tuckmanet Shoals a half mile to the east, and offshore in the deepest parts of the ocean the crushing undulations building into watery mountain ranges. She fell asleep with this music like a symphony eddying through her head. She felt her body break loose as she crossed the border into sleep and began to dream—surging, wonderful dreams of swimming deep beneath the surface. She felt the magnificence of her own body, its power as she melted into the water, becoming one with the sea and flowing through a dazzling underwater tapestry illuminated by the refractions of moonlight. At other times, the water was dark and yet occasionally shot through with odd, unexpected colors—a banner of seaweed glinting with a burnished luster.

Thick in the folds of sleep, she felt someone shaking her shoulder, bringing her up from the wonderful depths of her dreams and into her small square bedroom with its pale gray clapboard walls.

"May! May!" a voice said. She could feel the breath near her ear. She gasped and awakened suddenly. Rudd's face was close to hers. May pulled the bedclothes up to her chin.

"Sorry to come right into your room, but I knocked pretty hard. You didn't wake up. Anyhow, we done found him. He washed up a half hour ago."

She blinked again. It took her several seconds to comprehend what he was saying. May looked straight into his dark eyes. He had a scar above one eyebrow, and even now in winter his skin was a deep reddish bronze as if he never spent a day indoors. She had thought he was older. Apart from the crinkled lines that radiated out from the corners of his eyes, he looked perhaps twenty, but she knew he'd been fishing most likely all his life. This thought made her feel as if a chill wind brushed just beneath her skin.

She had grown up among fishermen. Eight out of every ten men in Bar Harbor were fishermen, so why should this one disturb her? He was certainly very attractive in his weathered way. She looked away from him quickly and got up from her bed. She had slept in her clothes.

"I have to go up to the lantern room to trim the wicks and wind the clockworks and bring my father something to eat," she said as she rushed toward the door.

"You're a busy lady." She felt a tiny pulse throb in her temple and averted her gaze. She was not sure she liked the term *lady*. It seemed constricting. *Like a girdle!* she suddenly thought, and almost laughed out loud. But she was well past her fifteenth birthday and it was not rare for girls in the fishing towns along the coast to marry at her age. She went to the stove and saw that it had a good fire going in it, and a kettle was about to boil.

Rudd was at her side. "I freshened it up."

"That was very kind of you," she said softly. "Thank you."

"Would you look at me when you thank me?" he asked.

She felt the blood rush to her face. She marveled that he was doing this—this courting, was it?—in front of Captain Haskell and a dead man. She turned her head slightly and suddenly realized that Captain Haskell was not there. Nor was the dead man on the cot. "Where are the others?" she asked.

"Well, the three half-drowned ones are still here. But Captain Haskell and Alfred, the first mate, done took the dead man into Bar Harbor and plan to sail back with a doctor for these three. He felt they were too sick to move right now. It's still cold out there, and sleeting."

"Yes, yes, of course." May had busied herself reheating a pot of leftover oatmeal.

"May!" a voice cawed.

May flinched. "It's my mother. I have to fetch her medicines."

"What's wrong with her?" Rudd asked.

Somehow these four words struck May as terribly funny. She almost began to laugh but turned to him with an odd smile that broadened until it seemed to illuminate her entire face. "She's sick," and then barely concealing a chuckle she added, "rather *she* would say so."

Rudd nodded and smiled, right into her smile. "Oh, I know the kind. I got an aunt like that and an older sister." For the first time May felt relaxed with him.

"You understand? You know what I am talking about?" He nodded. He did not smile. His face was serious. "Does it run in your family?" she asked. But to herself she was thinking, *I am not the only one.* It seemed almost miraculous to her that another person, this weathered sailor, had been bullied by another's illness.

He hesitated before speaking. "I think it runs up and down the coast of Maine and maybe all across New England for all I know. Women are fragile. They have complaints, weak constitutions, maybe."

"I'm not fragile," May replied, dumping a ladleful of oatmeal into a bowl.

"No. I can see that." His voice was taut. There was a sudden flickering in his eyes, not the flirtatious twinkle she had seen the previous night but a bright glitter that May found slightly unnerving.

THE CLOSET

HER MOTHER WAS PROPPED UP IN BED when May came with a tray covered with tablet boxes and tall glasses of water. On the small table beside the bed was another glass of water in which Hepzibah's false teeth floated eerily. For May they had a kind of animate life of their own, independent of her mother, as if on sudden provocation they could actually begin scolding May for some minor infraction.

"Good. You brought the smaller spoon." Hepzibah nodded at her daughter. "You can't really get these powders to properly mix with a big spoon. Hand me my specs, will you?"

"Yes, Ma." May set down the tray and walked to the dresser to fetch her mother's spectacles. Zeeba then set about mixing up the powders. Her face was suffused with an almost beatific look.

"I remember doing this so well for my mother and my grandmother. Powders were much coarser back then. Took longer to dissolve. But I learned, and oh, in that final illness of my mother's . . . oh, how she suffered! I never left her side."

May had heard the final illness stories of both women many times. Finally, when the powders had dissolved sufficiently, her mother looked up. "Have they left yet?" May bristled at the callousness of Zeeba's question.

"Three of the men, the ones that didn't die, are too sick to move right now."

Her mother's lips twitched and a grimace scored her face. "What are we running, then, a hospital instead of a lighthouse?"

"But, Ma. They're too sick. So the doctor's coming here."

The dark hole through which Hepzibah normally poked her words opened as her lips pulled back to reveal purple gums. She was smiling. A toothless smile. "The new doctor! Now, isn't that a bit of luck. The storm's done brought him to us!" She looked down and pressed her lips together.

Luck! Two men dead, another three nearly drowned! A tiny needle of malice pricked any patience May had left. "I hope the new doctor will be able to help Pa."

A darkness like storm clouds gathered in Hepzibah's face. "All he has to do is not touch that bottle," she snapped.

"He cut his hand and he did something to his hip. He can't walk."

Hepzibah made a sound halfway between a grunt and a snort. "Pass me my specs again, will you?" They were two inches away. She could have easily reached them herself, but May dutifully walked over to the side table. The teeth in the glass glared at her as she brought her mother her spectacles. "And my gargling cup." May sighed, handed her mother these articles, and left. She had to get out of this room.

It wasn't the solitude of their lives that bothered May, nor was it simply the stifling atmosphere of the lighthouse, but rather the silence that had grown up over the years. There was an insidious quality to it. Ironically, this silence spoke loudly and clearly to the bitterness, the resentment that had ripened and then rotted, eating away at both her parents.

The three of them lived on this windy rockbound island, and yet it was as if they needed to open every window and let scouring gusts blow through. But May knew that it wasn't wind that would vanquish the quiet but words. She was tired of the tyranny of this silence. In the past year she had sensed something changing in her. She felt a deepening intolerance for the way things had always been. May was known as an even-tempered girl. But she had been feeling slightly uneven recently, and the mysterious surge of the sea rising within her seemed to drive her more toward an edge she wanted to cross. This lighthouse was secure, safe, and boring. But May knew that she was on the brink of something rich, exciting, and yes, perhaps dangerous.

She went up the stairs with a bowl of oatmeal for her father. She had promised herself last night before finally falling asleep that she would ask him why he would never let her even go wading. She wasn't going to demand an explanation as she had burned to do the previous evening, and she certainly was not going to tell him that she thought she might have saved at least one of those men. But a quiet determination had rooted in her.

"Pa," she said as she entered the room. "How are you doing?"

"Quite a bit of pain in my hip. But I don't think anything is broken. Just stiffened up on me. How are the men downstairs that Captain Haskell picked up?"

"They seem settled for now. Captain Haskell sailed over to Bar Harbor to fetch the doctor to look at them. And he'll come up here and see about your hip and that cut."

"Oh, that will make your mother happy—a house call from the new doctor." He sighed, then laughed. "Don't think, though, that enough doctors could ever come calling to please your mother."

"'Spose you're right, Pa," May replied. She stifled the urge to ask him why he put up with her mother's behavior. There were so many times when she wished that Gar would just out-and-out get mad at Zeeba. But he never did. He would pour himself a little bit of whiskey, make a funny little grimace as he swallowed, and carry on.

"Pa, I brought you some oatmeal and some clean bandages for your cut, and spirits to wash it with."

"Well, I hate to tell you, de-ah, but seeing as it's my right hand that got so cut up, I'm afraid you're going to have to help me or I'll make a mess of myself."

"Don't you worry, Pa. I can do that."

"Serves me right, I suppose. You don't think that ship went down because of . . ."

May felt her chest tighten, but she forced herself to speak. "Don't say such a thing, Pa. It's not true. They could see the light. It's not our fault."

"*My* fault is what you mean."

"Quit it or I won't feed you another drop of this oatmeal." She smiled quickly at him. He chuckled. May sensed this was the time to ask her question. "Pa, how come you never let me get as much as a toe in the water?"

The color drained from Gar's face. "Wh-what are you talking about?"

"You know what I mean." May tried to say this in a half-teasing voice.

"After a night like this you want to know why I fear the sea for you?"

"Yes," May said, and looked at him directly, but he tried to avoid her eyes. He was looking around the watch room—every place except where his daughter was sitting beside him with the spoon of oatmeal held in midair.

There was a long silence. May noticed that Gar's eyes had settled on a small closet door that was always locked. After a moment, his gaze drifted back to her. May flinched when she noticed a shadow of sadness in his eyes.

"What's in that closet?"

The sadness vanished. "None of your business, miss!"

May was shocked and, at the same time, more intrigued than ever. She knew that he did not keep the key to the closet on the ring with the other keys of the lighthouse. This closet held secrets, and it was as forbidden to her as the water. In that moment the closet and the sea became linked in May Plum's mind. The words that Gar said next when he turned to May confirmed her thoughts.

"I been thinking, May, that maybe I could arrange a position for you off Egg Rock. You know, where you could make a bit of money."

"Where, Pa?"

"I thought maybe over in Bridgeton or Augusta," Gar said, looking away.

A quiet terror welled up inside her. Yes, she had wanted to get off this island, out of this house, but inland? There was something unimaginable, unthinkable, about not being in sight of the sea.

"Bridgeton! Augusta! Pa, that's so far. I don't want to go polishing some rich person's floor." Even if it meant escaping the silence and suffocation of the lighthouse, she could never move inland. To be so far from the sea would be another kind of suffocation.

Her father held up his hand. "Hold on, de-ah.

I don't see you polishing no old biddy's floors or sewing—though you are a good seamstress. But you're so good with book learning and numbers, better than me or your mother. I think you could be a teacher."

"But, Pa, I'm only fifteen. I haven't graduated school yet, and with the way the winter's been and me hardly ever getting across, it's going to take me an extra year at least."

But he wasn't listening to May at all. "Or maybe you could be a librarian like Miss Lowe. You'd like that, wouldn't you?"

This took May up short. A year ago she would have loved the notion of being a librarian. But now she was not so sure, especially if it took her to Bridgeton or Augusta, far from the sea.

"Maybe," she whispered sullenly.

"May?" New alarm sounded in her father's voice. "You seem a bit vexed."

Anger rose up in her. May wondered why her mother could always be "poorly," her father often drunk, but she herself had no right to feelings.

She squeezed her eyes shut and spoke. "Yes, Pa, I am feeling a mite vexed."

"Well, you'll get over it and be right as rain again. I suppose the strain and all."

She opened her eyes and looking at him took his hand. "No, Pa, I might not," she said softly, but there was a firmness in her voice. Gar stared at her as if, for a moment, his daughter had been replaced by a stranger. But even the look of hurt and confusion on his face wasn't enough to keep her from speaking.

"I do not see myself going inland to Bridgeton or Augusta, no matter if there were one hundred libraries where I could find employment. Not there!"

She stole a glance at the closet with its dwarfish door. She needed to find a way to open it. She was determined.

Voices could be heard downstairs. "The doctor must have arrived. I'll bring him up to see you as soon as he finishes examining the other men."

"And your mother, de-ah. Don't forget your mother. She will want a long consultation."

THE DOCTOR'S VISIT

HEPZIBAH PLUM ATTEMPTED to keep the new doctor, Lucius Holmes, by her bedside as long as possible.

"Fresh air! My goodness, Doctor Holmes, all we got around here is fresh air. I don't know what you're talking about."

"I think, Mrs. Plum, it would really help your gout." The doctor hesitated slightly. "Even more than this medicine."

Hepzibah Plum pulled herself higher on her pillows and leaned forward. "Doctor Holmes." She nearly spat out the two words. "I'll have you know that I know a thing or two about medical matters, too. This medicine treats the cause. Not just the symptom." She paused to let the power of this information and her knowledge sink in. "And I for one like to get to the cause and not merely the symptoms," she said smugly.

"Mrs. Plum, I do not dispute you, but in these days of modern medicine, it is possible to treat both."

But Hepzibah Plum had closed her ears to the doctor. "May!" she barked. "Fetch the chamber pot with my night urine. You'll see the crystals, Doctor Holmes."

May felt herself redden to the very roots of every hair on her head. She could not believe her mother was doing this, asking her to bring in the night pail to show someone else, even if that someone was a doctor. Hepzibah spent several minutes every morning examining her urine, but this was too much.

She decided to lie. "I'm sorry, Mother, but I already threw it out."

"You what?"

May might as well have said that she had thrown out the family silver had there been any.

"Well, Mother, there was so much going on here last night, what with the rescue and all. And then this morning I had to fix up a comfortable place for Pa since you felt there was not room here."

"Of course there wasn't room in this bed—not for two failing people," she muttered with barely concealed resentment.

Dr. Holmes's mouth settled into a grim line. May could almost feel the dislike flowing between the doctor and her mother. Hepzibah was not used to doctors like this. Old Doc Fletcher, who had died before Christmas, had been a master at humoring her mother. He used to marvel at Zeeba's descriptions of her condition, her thoughts about treatment. This doctor, although polite, was clearly less than impressed with her lengthy and detailed disquisitions on her various ailments. "My suggestion for some fresh air and exercise is based on evidence, Mrs. Plum, that mild physical activity can actually reduce the inflammation in the joints."

"You think walking on these will help them?" Hepzibah stuck one foot out from under the blankets to reveal an inflamed and knobby big toe that seemed rather like an accusatory eye glaring out from the bedclothes. "Talk to my toe, Doctor Holmes," Zeeba snarled. "See how it fails to preserve any sense of balance for me when I walk or stand for more than a few minutes."

"Perhaps if your daughter helped. Walked arm in arm with you a bit."

"Her! May? May's got her hands full as it is running the light and taking care of me and now her father with his so-called hip problem. You think she has time to waltz me around this island?" She paused.

"Yes, yes . . . I see the problem." For the first time Dr. Holmes seemed to have lost some of his composure. He ran his hands through his thinning hair, which was turning gray at the temples. He was always referred to as the "new young doctor," but May realized that was in comparison to Dr. Fletcher, who was almost ninety when he died. Dr. Holmes must be close to fifty. He was not what one would ever call a handsome man, but there was something very appealing about his manner that made up for what might constitute any flaws in his physical appearance. His nose did seem a bit long, and his eyes drooped somewhat at the corners. His ears were rather large, and yet all of these features came together in a pleasing manner.

"Well, I'm glad you do!" Hepzibah said in a calmer voice. "I have complications. I have for a lifetime. And with them come other complications. Why, I doubt May'll be able to go back to school this month."

"Mother, I've been out for three weeks because of weather."

She shot May a dark look. "Well, your father should've thought about that before he—" But before she could finish the doctor broke in.

"Yes, Mrs. Plum, of course. You're right." May felt her heart sink. Why had the doctor given in so quickly? But just as she gave up hope, he spoke. "But, Mrs. Plum, a girl has to get out."

Hepzibah jerked her head up. Her nearly black eyes seemed to spring out from their sockets. Dr. Holmes might just as well have said, "A girl needs to go to the moon."

"What in the name of Pete are you talking about?"

"A young healthy girl cannot be confined all the time to take care of sick people."

Hepzibah's mouth gaped open, then closed slightly and opened again. It was as if her lips could not grab hold of the shape of the words to respond.

Dr. Holmes turned and said, "Mrs. Plum, I shall send you some more medicine for your gout." In a lower voice he added, "May, meet me at the dock. I'd like to speak to you."

May saw the doctor waiting at the end of the dock, where Captain Haskell had tied up. To her surprise, the men had just finished loading the survivors on the boat.

"I thought they were too ill to move," May said as she walked up to the doctor.

Dr. Holmes turned to her. "I think you have your hands full enough. We'll get these fellows across all right." He gave a slight cough and seemed to be studying the barnacles on the pilings. "I meant what I said back there in the lighthouse. You need to get out." May looked down at the toes of her shoes. She had not put on her rubberized weather boots, and the water was slopping over the edge of the float.

"Listen to me!" There was a sudden urgency in the doctor's voice that May found alarming. "Your mother is not weak. She is strong in many ways that you might not suspect." May was startled. And she saw that Dr. Holmes was somewhat taken aback by his own outburst when he looked at her. "I don't want to worry you. But although she has 'complications' as she calls them, well, how to put this?" He suddenly seemed very unsure of himself. "Her illnesses cannot, should not, be the center of your life." He paused at this point. "Is her illness the center of your father's life as well?" May felt as if the doctor and she were speaking some sort of code. Yet there was a feeling of relief just in being asked, the first tiny crack in the lighthouse silence.

"Well, my father—it's not easy for him with her, and he does drink a bit, sir," she replied hesitantly.

Dr. Holmes looked at her. "Perhaps I could find you someone to help out here. My wife might know someone."

May shook her head. "Oh, I don't think so, Doctor Holmes. We don't have money for that kind of thing, and besides, my mother wouldn't stand for it. She's very particular."

"Well, May, you have a life, too. Remember that."

"Yes, sir."

6

A YEARNING DETECTED

Lucius Holmes watched as the island receded into the distance. May's dilemma was a haunting one. At the very core of it was her mother's selfishness, combined with her father's drinking. In addition, he sensed Edgar Plum's absolute passivity. All of this did not make for a promising situation for May. He could imagine her life on this tiny barren island too easily. The isolation, the loneliness. And that mother! A tyrannical, vicious woman.

As he watched he saw May climb to a promontory and look out to the east, toward The Bones and beyond to the boundless ocean. She leaned into the wind. Her red hair began to escape from its pins, and tendrils flared into the gusts like licks of fire. *Yearning,* that was the word that came to mind as he watched her. She bent to this breeze as if she were longing to be transported to some invisible place. Did she expect the breeze to carry her there? Did she ache to throw herself on a gust and join the squawking seagulls that wheeled in the sky overhead? No! Not air but water! The sea. She was looking straight down into the churning waters of the sea.

He turned to Captain Haskell, who was at the helm. "I am new here. This is the first time I've met the Plums. What do you know about them?"

"Not much to tell, Doctor. They married late. Gar is a nice enough fellow. He'd been engaged to a pretty girl. Polly Bunker. But on the eve of their wedding Polly took sick, and within two weeks she was dead."

"What about Mrs. Plum?"

"She was Hepzibah Greenlaw. No one ever expected her to marry. She'd spent most of her life taking care of her mother, who was . . . well, frail, and her grandmother as well. A few weeks after Polly died Zeeba's mother went as well. I think Zeeba set her sights on Gar at Polly's funeral, to tell you the truth. She rarely left her own house, but on that day she got a young girl to come in and mind her mother, who was failing fast. She went to the service and then showed up with a kettle of chowder at Polly's parents' house that evening. I was there with my wife, Emma. Emma saw the whole thing. Hepzibah went right up to Gar and said, 'You got to eat.' Then Emma said that Zeeba—that's what everyone calls her, Zeeba—said the queerest thing. She said, 'Even grief has to eat.' Like it's a cat or something that you have to feed. Have you ever heard the likes of it?"

Lucius Holmes shook his head. *Not exactly*, he thought, but it made a strange kind of sense. There was just one flaw in the peculiar statement—Hepzibah had used the wrong word. It was not grief that had to be fed, it was anger. There was a dreadful logic that drove this woman. She had spent her youth serving invalids—her mother and her grandmother.

And when they died it became her turn. She did not seek love, she did not seek a companion but a caregiver. And this logic could be passed down from generation to generation, just like a hereditary disease. There was truly someone to save here and it was not Hepzibah Plum. It was May. He did not want May Plum to become the next victim.

"Folks were taken by surprise when she had May."

"Why's that?"

"Well, she was old for one thing, and they'd been married quite a while, and her being frail as she is with all her complications. It was a pretty bad winter and all, so they hadn't gotten into town. Anyhow, come spring they show up with little May. She was born, they said, at a time when there was no way a doctor could go out there to help Zeeba, but she seemed to do fine."

⚜ ⚜ ⚜

Lucius Holmes fell silent and looked as Egg Rock receded. He could still see the young girl's figure on the promontory, and even from this distance he could feel her yearning. She could have been a figurehead stretching out from the bow of a sailing vessel, cutting the wind, at one with the rhythms of the sea, a dancer on the cresting waves.

SPRING 1899

"YOU HORRID GIRL!"

THE DAYS HAD BRIGHTENED and the seas had calmed. There was at last a true hint of the coming spring in the air, but in the month or so since the disaster on The Bones, May's life had become as monotonous and as dreary as the darkest days of winter. Her mother had let her go to school only one day. Her excuse was that until May's father had recovered enough to climb the stairs they could not risk her going ashore. Edgar had protested vigorously to no avail. It was true that he was still quite lame, but he argued that this was no reason why May shouldn't be allowed to go to school.

They were having one such quarrel now. "But, Mother," May said in response to her father's pleas and Zeeba's refusal. "Even Doctor Holmes said a girl needs to get out."

"Yes, and he told me that I needed fresh air and look where we live! The man's a durned fool. And that medicine he sent out on the mail boat ain't worth the bottle it came in. We don't need another disaster here like the ship that fetched up on The Bones. We'll lose the lighthouse—and then where will we go? We're poor. Your father drinks."

"He has not had a drop since that night, Mother, and you know it!" May screamed. She had never shouted like this at Zeeba. It felt as if she had unleashed a great gale from deep inside her that had been brewing for years.

Hepzibah looked at her daughter with shock, and then quickly her face darkened. Anger rose in her like a coiled viper. "You horrid girl! Where did you come from? Where did he get you?" She turned to Gar. "You—you—couldn't ever forget Polly, could you?"

"What are you talking about?" May looked at her mother and then at her father.

"Don't, Zeeba! Don't!" her father blurted out as he collapsed into his chair.

"Don't what? What is she saying, Pa?" She felt something crack inside her. "Where did I come from?" She turned her head again toward Zeeba. "You're my mother!"

Hepzibah's face seemed to relax, and a smirk crawled across it. "You want to tell her, Gar?" Her voice was cold, but it was clear she was enjoying May's confusion.

"Tell me what?" May shouted.

"You're not mine." Hepzibah said quietly, looking down at a medical journal she had been reading.

"What do you mean? I—I—don't understand."

"I did not give birth to you."

"What?" May's chin trembled, and her mouth seemed to have trouble forming the single word.

"Do you honestly think that this poor failing body of mine could ever give birth to a child, let alone one as—as"—Hepzibah struggled to say the words—"as healthy as you, as strong, as robust as you!" She spoke this last part as if it were the vilest imprecation.

"Wh-where did I come from?" May looked at her father. "Who's Polly?" She was nearly staggering as she stood. It felt as if the ground beneath her were shaking. If these two were not her parents, who were? She was caught in a firestorm of confusing emotions—rejection and yet an odd sense of relief. She could accept Hepzibah not loving her. She probably never had. But she couldn't bear the thought of losing Gar.

Her father stood up, and although he was still lame, it was the most erect she had seen him since before the shipwreck. He walked directly over to Hepzibah and spoke. "It is not just me. I am not the only one who could not forget Polly. You couldn't either, Zeeba. You!"

"Down the coast, he always told me," Hepzibah sneered. "Found you down the coast."

"I don't understand this. Not at all. Someone please explain where I come from?"

Gar limped over to May and put his arm around her. "A woman, a young woman, not Polly. It couldn't be. I had been engaged to Polly but she died ten years before you were ever born. But she"—he nodded at Zeeba—"never got over the fact she wasn't first choice."

"That ain't true, Gar, and you know it!"

"It is true, Hepzibah. You're so eaten up with jealousy over a dead woman you can't do simple figuring. You know when I walked in here with May it was 1883. You know Polly died in 1873. How the devil could she be Polly's?" May gasped.

"The devil—exactly!" Hepzibah's eyes gleamed, and she turned her head slowly toward May. "I always knew there was something unnatural about that girl."

"What?" May's voice was tight with alarm. "You think . . ." But it was as if the words evaporated.

"You'll never know what I think . . . think of you or him." Zeeba jerked her head toward Gar but kept her eyes clamped on May. Gar stepped to the side, as if to protect her from Zeeba's glare.

"You listen to me, May. A woman down toward Crockett Cove, past Winter Harbor, was your mother. She died giving birth. There weren't no one to care for you. I offered to take you back here. I thought it would please Zeeba." He paused and cupped her chin lightly in his hand. "And it has pleased me deeply."

"B-b-but," May stammered. She couldn't bring herself to say the words that screamed in her mind. *You're not my real father.* She felt a dark hole opening up in her. It was as if she were missing her core. She swayed slightly and put a hand on the back of a chair to steady herself. "What happened to the father?" May asked.

"Yes, what happened?" Hepzibah said in a flat voice.

Now Gar turned and looked at Hepzibah. "Your mother has had this notion that I am your father. But it ain't so, May. And I am sorry. For truly I would love to be your real father. I love you as if I were."

May moved away from the chair and then back to where her father stood. Taking her father's face in both her hands she said, "No, Pa, you love me better than my so-called real father, for he left. You love me like a true father."

There were teardrops trembling in the rims of his eyes. In the glistening wetness she saw the sphere that held her own reflection—her own quivering face. Was Gar no part of her? Did she belong to no one? May felt as if she were sliding off a cliff and was tumbling in a free fall through that dark nothingness of her missing center. She shut her eyes tight for several seconds as if anticipating the impact.

In those seemingly endless seconds the image of the small door came to her. She had not thought of that tiny closet in the watch room but once or twice since the morning after the shipwreck. She had no idea where the key was and had more or less given up on trying to find it. But now she was certain that the secret of her birth was hidden in the closet that Gar kept so carefully locked all these years.

She vowed to find that key, no matter what. Her father could still barely make it up the stairs. She spent more time than ever alone in the watch room. She might never have such an opportunity again. For the first time she thought of her father's infirmity as a blessing.

A VISITOR

MAY WAS HALFWAY UP THE STAIRS to the watch room to search for the key to the closet when she heard a sharp rap on the door. "Who's that?" Hepzibah said, half rising from her rocker.

"I'll get it," she heard her father say. Then seconds later, Gar called up the winding stairs, "Someone here to see you, May."

"Me?"

"Yep. That fellow Rudd from the night of the storm."

Now of all times?

"All right. Tell him I'll be out in a minute, Pa."

She quickly slipped into her bedroom and went to the mirror set on her bureau. She was a mess. The incredible revelations minutes before had left their mark on her. She repinned her hair. It didn't help much. Her skin was all blotchy, but the blotches were in the wrong places. Her cheeks were pale and her eyes were rimmed with dim lavender circles! She pinched her cheeks to get some color in them, took a deep breath, and tried to look composed as she walked to the front door of the lighthouse.

Rudd Sawyer leaned against the jamb, filling the frame. He radiated an unassailable confidence, almost a sense of ownership. If someone didn't know better, he might have thought Rudd was the proprietor of the lighthouse and even the entire island.

May hadn't realized quite how tall he was or how broad his shoulders were. With the warmer weather he wasn't wearing a jacket. His collar was open and his sleeves were rolled up. His forearms had curls of hair slightly lighter than the hair on his head. His fingers tapped the doorjamb casually as if to suggest he'd been waiting a while, maybe too long.

"Hello, May."

"Rudd!"

"None other." A wide smile cut his face. "Does there have to be a shipwreck to see you again?"

"Oh—oh—oh, no, of course not." She was dying to get up to the watch room. As handsome as he was, Rudd constituted a distraction more than anything else.

"You gonna invite me in?"

"Uh . . . well, no. But . . . we could take a walk." She could not let this young man come into the lighthouse, not with her mother glaring away. And certainly not after what had just transpired. In the scant minutes between Hepzibah's revelation and the time Rudd had knocked on the door, May's whole world had changed. There had hardly been a moment to recover. She might not even *want* to recover if it meant trying to make amends with Zeeba. *Zeeba!* In her mind she had just called her mother Zeeba. She had done this without even thinking.

She now heard Zeeba calling out from her bedroom. "Who's that at the door, May? Who's there?" May did not reply but merely turned to Rudd and said, "Come along, we can walk down to the beach."

⚓ ⚓ ⚓

A few minutes later they were standing on a small crescent of sand looking out to sea. "They don't look fierce at all, do they, in this calm?" Rudd nodded toward The Bones.

"It's nearly high tide. In another quarter of an hour you won't be able to see them," she said. It seemed amazing to her that she was speaking to him almost normally. She had the strange sensation that she had stepped out of her own body and was walking along beside it on the beach, watching herself listen, talk, and nod or shake her head at the right times.

"Did the new chimney come in yet?" he asked.

"Not supposed to come in until tomorrow to the chandlery."

"Well, then, if you pick it up you can come to the dance." He flashed her a quick smile.

"What dance?"

"Dance at the Odd Fellows Hall. They used to call it the end of the line gale dance."

"What?" May tipped her head and looked at him questioningly. He was really asking her to a dance? She suddenly realized that her mouth was hanging open. She must look utterly stupid. But he wasn't looking at her mouth.

"Do you know how green your eyes are?"

"No! I don't make a habit of looking at myself in a mirror all day long." She ducked her chin down. What kind of question was that?

"Well, they are."

"What's an end of the line gale dance?" May asked without meeting Rudd's eyes.

"Line gales—you know what they are."

"Yes, they come in March, around the time of the equinox."

"Equinox—my, my." He raised one eyebrow a bit as if he were impressed, but she was sure she caught a glint of something close to mockery in his eyes.

"What do you mean, 'my, my'? There's nothing 'my, my' about the equinox. It's when the sun crosses the equator and the length of days equals the nights," she said matter-of-factly.

"You must have a lot of book learning."

"I read, but I also know how much kerosene we burn in the lantern room. Less and less after the spring equinox." She paused, then added, "That's not book learning. That's just living."

He looked at her and laughed. "Well, it's the end of March, almost April, and those line gales are usually finished by then. So they have a celebration. How about doing a bit of living?"

May smiled to herself. *"A bit of living."* It sounded good. A bit of living as opposed to a bit of slow asphyxiation by Hepzibah. *Am I starting to hate her?* May wondered. She looked at Rudd and grinned broadly. "Oh, I'm all for that. All for living." She blushed. Did she seem too eager? She wanted to tease him a bit. Didn't girls sometimes do that?

"But maybe they should delay the dance," May said, and kicked a stone with the toe of her shoe.

"Why?"

"Just to be on the safe side," she replied.

"Just to be on the safe side? What are you talking about?" Rudd laughed.

"You don't want to jinx it by having the dance too soon. Have it in May, when you know the line gales are over." She wished she didn't sound so serious. She wished she didn't state facts so stolidly. But she had no gift for light, flirtatious conversation. This was what came from being sealed up in a lighthouse.

"But there's a May Day dance in May, and of course you have to come to that one. I mean, May being your name and all. And another one in June."

May tossed a beach pebble into the surf. "But I don't want to jinx anything. I don't want a line squall driving a ship onto The Bones."

"Oh, I think except for that storm last month you've done pretty well out here on Egg Rock. I'd say you got Saint Anthony keeping an eye on you."

An image flashed in May's mind: the slightly tipped carved figure of the saint on that night of her father's accident. Was it possible that this was where the key to the small closet had been hidden?

May jumped up.

"I have to go, Rudd. Just remembered that I haven't trimmed the wicks . . . and—and—"

"Will you come to the dance?"

She was about to say she had to ask her mother, but then she remembered that Zeeba wasn't her mother. What did she care what Zeeba thought? She would never forget how Zeeba's eyes had gleamed when she had spat out those three words *"the devil—exactly!"* If she was a horrid girl she might as well start acting like one, and going to the dance without permission would constitute colossal disobedience. "Yes, I'll come! But I can't get home too late."

"Don't worry. I'll get Gus's skiff, the one I got to get out here today, and sail you there and back."

"Gus?"

"Gus Bridges, captain of the *Sea Hound*. I'm working for him now."

"You're not with Captain Haskell anymore?"

"Not for now. He just lobsters. I like going offshore for sword. Whole different game." His eyes glittered fiercely. "Going after swordfish—now, that's fishing!

And that's where the money is! Catching the big ones."

"Oh," May said. For some reason she found his words unsettling. "Well, I really have to go," she said, thinking of the little closet in the watch room. She felt as if it were waiting for her.

THE KEY

THE FIGURE OF SAINT ANTHONY was exactly as she remembered, tipped slightly to one side. And now as she stood just beneath it, between the Fresnel lens and the panel that separated the two east-facing windows, she could see something else she had never noticed. There was a faint seam in the panel. When she reached up and took down the Saint Anthony figure she saw that there was the outline of a rectangle with a tiny hole in the center. She narrowed her eyes. The hole was no bigger in diameter than an embroidery needle. She took out a hairpin and stuck it into the hole, wiggled it a bit, then gave a gentle tug. The rectangle came out and behind it hung a brass key. *This is it!* she thought. She took the key, and even just holding it gave her a thrill. Yet as she crept down the ladder, the fluttering in her stomach hardened into a knot. Gar had gone to a great deal of trouble to hide the key. What could be the reason for all the secrecy?

She reached the service area and scurried over to the small closet. She fit the key into the keyhole, then turned it, praying that the door wouldn't creak. It did not but seemed to glide open with very little effort on her part. A wonderful fragrance floated from the dark shadows of the closet. It reminded her of something, something she had forgotten entirely.

She had been barely conscious of squeezing her eyes shut when she first opened the small door and inhaled the wonderful rimy sea smell. Now she was almost afraid to open them, but she did and peered inside. There was a chest. It looked like an ordinary sea chest, but then she noticed the carving of three small mermaids on the front. Carefully she pulled the chest from the closet. She did not want to make any noise. She ran her hand over the letters carved on the lid of the chest—HMS *Resolute*. *It must be British*, May thought. HMS stood for Her Majesty's Ship.

May ran her hand over the carving of the three mermaids. As she traced over their tails with her finger, May felt a rush of feelings—a strange sort of peacefulness as if something had been found, and yet a deep pang of loss—something gone, irretrievably gone. She was engulfed by an impenetrable isolation, a feeling of being cut off from everything she had ever known or trusted and yet at the same time connected to something vital, hauntingly familiar, and intensely intimate.

Cautiously she lifted the lid of the sea chest and found herself peering into a disappointing emptiness. She was not sure what she had expected, but despite its depth there were only a few articles. A neatly folded, tattered-looking gray blanket, a piece torn from a newspaper, a yellow envelope addressed to Mr. Edgar Plum, and a folded navigational chart.

The emptiness of the chest shocked her, embarrassed her, mocked her hopes. These paltry articles seemed like shabby relics of the Plums' mundane lighthouse existence. How could they offer clues into the great mystery that she felt at the very center of her being?

May took out the gray blanket first and pressed it to her nose. It was as if she were inhaling the scent that came from the very heart of the sea. Yet there was another scent there. Something warm and almost milky. She had not realized it, but tears had begun to roll down her face. She carefully unfolded the blanket. It had several holes and in many other places it had begun to unravel. She was just about to ask herself why anyone would keep such a thing when she spotted a red glint enmeshed in the threads of one frayed patch. She took the same hairpin she had used before and plucked at the bright red thread. "But it's not a thread!" she whispered to herself. It was hair. Her own hair, yet it was infinitely softer. Baby hair! Was this the blanket her father had brought her back in from her dead mother down the coast? It must be. But why would he keep it locked away? Her face was wet with tears. "Why, Pa? Why?" she whispered to herself, and rocked back and forth, clutching the blanket.

Reluctantly she set the blanket back in the chest just as she had found it and took out the letter, dated

June 20, 1883. The return address was the Revenue Cutter Service.

Dear Mr. Plum,

In regard to your inquiry concerning the latitude and longitude of the sinking of the HMS Resolute, *we do not have a precise position but we do have coordinates for wreckage from the vessel that was found drifting in a north and easterly direction. Some spars were picked up some months after the storm by the Revenue Service cutter* George P. Marshall *at 41°36′ N and 70°36′ W on April 19, 1883. An overturned lifeboat was found south of Martha's Vineyard, April 30 of this year by the fishing sloop* Abigail *out of Nantucket. Sundry wooden fragments believed to be from the ship have continued to be found over the summer. No bodies have as yet been recovered. It is doubtful that they would this long after the disaster. The HMS Resolute was commanded by Captain Walter Lawrence of the Admiralty, a distinguished officer in Her Majesty's service for over fifteen years.*

At this time I have no more information. Perhaps by autumn, when the northeasters begin to blow, more information shall be yielded. Please feel free to write again.

Most sincerely yours,
Lieutenant Michael Ramsey,
Newport, RI Station of the United States Revenue Cutter Service

May read the letter again, staring down at the words on the page, and wondered why Gar had written. Why did he want to know where the *Resolute* had sunk? Carefully, May replaced the letter, then reached in for the chart. When she unfolded it she realized that there were two charts. One depicted Georges Bank and the Nantucket Shoals. The second chart went from Boston Light to Cape Ann: the coastline south of Maine. She saw faint pencil markings. There was an x and a question mark on the first chart near a region in the Nantucket Shoals called Cultivator Shoals at 41°20' N and 68°12' W. She brought the chart closer and squinted. May was not ignorant of navigational charts. She understood that the tiny numbers marked the depths in fathoms and that the direction and the average velocities of currents were indicated by the purple arrows. Someone had drawn lines extending out from these arrows as if to suggest a continuation of a current.

On the first chart there were two more x's without question marks—one on the Nantucket Shoals and one precisely at the longitude/latitude of 41°36' N and 70°36' W, the location referred to in the letter. From the position of these three sets of x's, lines were drawn that followed the current arrows. It made a fairly tight circle. But then she saw another very dim line, hardly visible, that stretched toward the north and east. When she took out the second chart she could see that a similar line had been drawn picking up where the line on the first chart had ended at Boston Light. The pencil markings suggested an invisible current that might flow down east, toward Maine. She moved her finger along the chart, and there she found a single x on Simon's Ledge. "Simon's Ledge," she whispered. "Why?"

She was sure the charts and the blanket were all somehow connected to her and her birth mother. It was a strange puzzle, but the central piece, the keystone, was the strand of red hair that wove it all together. The knowledge dawned on her slowly, like a radiance beginning to illuminate her brain. *All of these things are linked to me!*

May put away the articles in the chest just as she had found them. She even poked the little strand of hair back into the frayed blanket. Despite the lack of real evidence, the very air within the chest seemed to swirl with whispers, with deep, rich secrets. She lay her cheek against the lid as if to listen. Then she got up and placed the key back into the panel behind the Saint Anthony figure and gave the saint a slight pat to thank him, although she was not sure for what. The chest only compounded the mystery for her. She had to figure out the meaning of the things in the chest. Figure out where she had come from and where she might go. If she didn't belong here with Hepzibah and Gar, she must belong somewhere.

After replacing the key, May set herself to washing the windows of the lantern room. It was one of those mindless tasks that freed her brain to think.

While she washed the panes, she reviewed the paltry information she had picked up. Why was her father so afraid of her entering the water? It was a real fear; he had threatened—albeit mildly—to send her to Bridgeton or Augusta. Her second question— the most important one—Who was her birth mother? Was it some woman who had died down the coast or beyond Winter Harbor? And this led to the third question—Where was she born?

Her mind went back to the sea chest, beguiling in its emptiness. Gar must have been figuring out the path, the tracks that the wreckage of the *Resolute* had taken. Her father hadn't lied exactly when he had said she had been brought from down the coast — but it was far beyond Crockett Cove. And far from land. If she wanted to discover where she really came from, she needed to find the wrecked ship.

AN EXTRAORDINARY IDEA

No one was at the desk when May came through the door of the library. She'd picked up the new chimney and rushed across town.

"Miss Lowe," she called out. She was impatient. She had thought all night about how she would go about her research and was eager to start. It was exciting. For the first time ever, May was embarking on a voyage—she who had never gone any farther than Bath.

She heard a rustling in the back.

"Be right with you!" A few seconds later Jean Lowe came through a door behind her desk, carrying a stack of books.

"May, how good to see you! I heard about your

father's injury. Quite a night you had out there when that schooner snagged on The Bones!"

"Yes, quite a night." Although May was not so much thinking of that evening but of yesterday. The list of questions in her head seemed so big and unanswerable. But she had awakened that morning with a new set of questions, specific questions about the faint pencil marks on the charts.

"Miss Lowe, do you have any books about currents?"

"Currents?"

"Yes, ocean currents and winds?"

"Now, how odd you should ask." Miss Lowe pushed up her spectacles, which had slipped down her nose, then scratched her head. Her fingers disappeared into the frizzy gray mass of hair that was pinned up and seemed to hover above her head like a storm cloud suddenly rolled in from offshore. "There was just a young man in here earlier asking for books on the same subject. I directed him to Bowditch's book of pilot charts over at the chandlery and got him a few other volumes. But I entirely forgot about one that would have been helpful to him and I guess to you." Her blue eyes sparkled from behind the lenses of her spectacles. "Maury!"

"Who?"

"Matthew Fontaine Maury, really much better than the pilot charts I recommended for that young Harvard man. He's here conducting some research — tides, stars, and many things I don't understand." She waved her hand as if to dismiss an immense body of knowledge that was hopelessly beyond her. "Follow me." Miss Lowe scurried around the end of the desk, and May followed her to the far side of the library. Miss Lowe turned into an aisle and began threading her way through two tall rows of bookshelves. She was talking a mile a minute as May followed.

"You see, Matthew Fontaine Maury was a Christian naval officer from somewhere down south. Virginia, maybe. He loved to read the Bible. But he had some doubts about how accurate it really was, particularly when it came to matters of the ocean and the winds. Could you rely on it word for word? You know, the biblical references to the sea." She paused and began to walk slower as she looked up and ran her hands lightly over a row of books at shoulder height, whispering softly to herself—"Celestial navigation, compass boxing." There were indeed dozens of books on both sides of the aisle pertaining to maritime subjects.

"Ah!" she exclaimed. "Here it is. *The Physical Geography of the Sea and Its Meteorology* by Matthew Fontaine Maury." May could hear the little crick of dried glue as she opened the book. "Mercy! I don't think anyone has checked this book out in over thirty years!"

"You mean I'm the first?" May asked.

"I expect so! The Harvard fellow would have been the first if I had thought of it. But you have the honor."

"He's from the university?" May had trouble imagining some Harvard man wandering through the dusty stacks of the Bar Harbor library.

"Yes, my dear. You beat a Harvard man to the punch on this." She laughed. "My fault, I guess. Oh, I tell you, my memory!" She ran her fingers through the foam of gray hair as if to jostle her brains a bit.

May felt a little quiver of excitement run through her at the thought of being the first person to have read the book in such a long time. It was as if the book had a secret waiting just for her.

"You see, May—here is the biblical passage that started Mr. Maury off on his search for the tracks of the sea."

"The tracks of the sea—" May repeated the words in a whisper. There was a resonance to them that was almost mystical.

"'Whatsoever passeth through the paths of the seas,'" Miss Lowe read.

"Psalm eight," May said.

"Exactly. The psalmist was marveling at the limitless grandeur of God's creation. Now, Maury felt if the psalmist said there were paths of the seas, then by gum there must be. So he set out to find them!" Miss Lowe looked up, her bright blue eyes twinkling.

May felt herself begin to grin. "May I read it here?" she asked.

"Well, of course, but you know you can check it out and take it back to Egg Rock with you."

"Yes, but I'm not going back for a while."

Miss Lowe blinked with surprise. "Oh, really?" May seldom spent much time in Bar Harbor. Especially on a Saturday, when there was no school.

"I'm going to the dance—the end of the line gales dance," May answered, dropping her eyes.

"Why, May Plum, good for you. I wondered why you were so dressed up."

"Oh, it's not much," May said, smoothing her hand over the front of the calico fitted jacket that she was wearing with a soft blue wool skirt. She had sewn a flounce of lace around the collar, which gave it a festive appearance. It was cheap lace, as Zeeba had reminded her at the time. It had edged a tablecloth someone had given Zeeba as a wedding gift and had ripped off after a few washings. But May hoped she looked better than when she had last seen Rudd. It was so easy, she thought, for boys. They never looked poorly if they were basically handsome. They didn't have to fool with their hair, and because they grew beards, or even if they were smooth-shaven, their skin never looked blotchy if they had been upset, as she certainly had been when Rudd called.

"And that locket—so pretty."

"My father gave it to me for my last birthday." May touched it lightly. It was silver with a filigree of inter-twining vines.

"Well, I won't ask you what you keep in it."

"Nothing, Miss Lowe."

"When you do find something to keep in it, that will be your secret. You always have to keep a little something just for yourself, May."

She thought of the sea chest, nearly empty yet silently shuddering, dark with its secrets. The empti-ness of the locket seemed in some way to echo the aching hollowness within her.

"Here you go." Miss Lowe handed the book to May. "Why don't you curl up in your favorite spot?" She nodded toward a back corner of the library where there was a little window seat. "Make yourself at home. I have to leave in an hour or so, but you can stay here until the dance starts if you'll just turn the latch behind you when you leave. Of course, by that time it might be too dark to read. There's a small oil lamp you can use if you promise to turn down the wick and make sure it's all the way out before you go."

"Oh, I surely will, Miss Lowe. This is so kind of you!"

"Not at all, May." She smiled, and there was just a trace of worry that seemed to dim the blueness of her eyes for a moment. "I'm so happy to see you getting out. Now that the weather is nice, I hope I'll see you more."

"You will!" May said brightly. The words Rudd had spoken to her came back. "I'm going to start doing a bit of living!"

Miss Lowe cocked her head, then nodded vigorously. "Good for you, May, good for you!"

May settled herself happily into the window seat, opened the book, and began reading the first chapter: "The Sea and the Atmosphere."

"The two oceans of air and water: Our planet is invested with two great oceans; one visible, the other invisible; one underfoot, the other overhead; one entirely envelops it, the other covers about two-thirds of its surface. All the water of one weighs about four hundred times as much as the air of the other."

Two oceans, May thought. *What an extraordinary idea!*

❧　❧　❧

Some of the book May didn't understand and some she did. But she loved the adventure of figuring it out. This was personal to her, much more vital than learning how to diagram a sentence or memorizing a poem. She had liked learning in school. She was a good student, but she had never felt such urgency to understand as she did with Mr. Maury and his book. If she could understand Maury, the links between those disparate objects in the chest might become clear—clear as sunlit water.

She began to grasp the interplay between the bottom of the lighter "ocean," the one of air, and the surface of the second one, of water—the currents of both and how they each affected the other. Maury referred to two main wind currents—ones that flowed from both poles of the earth, each toward the equator. But within and between these two main currents of air was a patchwork quilt of smaller currents, "bands" he called them, of wind and water, sometimes calm and sometimes boisterous. And there were rules that governed it all—laws of physics and geography. These laws functioned somewhat like clockworks and ruled the pendulums of the wind and water of two great oceans—the invisible and the visible.

May was interested specifically in the small gyres of circulating air and water currents that worked along the New England coast, for those were what might explain the *x*'s that Edgar Plum had marked on the two charts.

Absorbed in the book, May completely lost track of time. It was only the guttering flame in the lantern that alerted her to how long she had been reading. The dance must have already started. She heard a knocking at the front door of the library, then the creak of the door as it opened.

"I hope I'm not too late. You still open, Miss Lowe?"

May shut the book and walked to the front with the kerosene lamp.

This must be the Harvard man, she thought. He was holding the Bowditch pilot guide to his chest. She recognized the cover. Her father kept the same one on the shelf in the parlor. When he spotted May, his gray eyes widened with surprise. He tipped his head and seemed to be trying to read the title of the book May was still clutching to her chest.

"Oh!" There was a sharpness in this single word. "It appears that Maury has quite the following in Maine."

"I believe this is the book that Miss Lowe forgot to tell you about. I—I—" May stammered. "I was looking for books about currents, too."

"Yes," he said. "*The Physical Geography of the Sea*—not all that popular, but you apparently found your way to it." He raised one eyebrow slightly as if to wonder at a simple island girl's interest in such a book. He paused and thrust out his hand. "I'm Hugh Fitzsimmons."

"The Harvard man."

He looked down and gave a slight cough. "Yes, among other things."

"You're a student, Mr. Fitzsimmons?"

"A graduate student in astronomy. But please just call me Hugh. And what is your name?"

"May Plum." She swallowed. "Miss Lowe said you were here to conduct some research."

"Yes. I am exploring the gravitational pull of the moon on the tides, looking for a correspondence with the transits of the stars. It's somewhat complicated—the theory."

Too complicated for me, I suppose, May thought, somewhat indignantly.

"The analogies between what's up there"—he pointed vaguely with his thumb—"and—"

"The invisible ocean," May said quickly.

"You know your Maury, I see," Hugh replied, a small smile crossing his face. "Tell me, May, have you any thoughts about Maury's comments on the Pleiades?"

May had the distinct impression that he was quizzing her, as if he couldn't believe a local girl could really understand Maury's work. She cleared her throat and then looking him straight in the eye began.

"I think Mr. Maury uses Scripture to explain how those seven stars might be the center, like poles, around which Earth and all the planets move."

He nodded. "He uses, I believe, quotes from the book of Job as well as Ecclesiastes. But it is the reference to Job—'Canst thou bind the sweet influences of Pleiades'—that he really uses to explain this movement. In particular he views Alcyone in the Pleiades as the pole star. He has, of course, been criticized mightily for this." He paused and looked at May expectantly.

"I have no idea if he is right or wrong. But it seems that his knowledge of the currents of the visible ocean is fair," she replied.

"Just fair?" His dark eyebrows shot up and, for a moment, she worried she had said something wrong. But then his face broke into a broad smile. Deep creases appeared on either side of his mouth and his eyes like parentheses. "Well, as I said, you certainly know your Maury."

"I've been reading all afternoon. I should have learned something by now."

He chuckled slightly. "What drew you to him in the first place?"

How could she answer his question? She didn't dare tell him about the shipwreck of the *Resolute* and her suspicions about its connection to her own origins. She tried to sound casual. "Well, I do live in a lighthouse. There was a bad wreck end of last winter. A coastal schooner fetched up on some ledges we call The Bones. Men died. I started wondering about the currents. It was stormy, but I started to think there might be a current that drove that ship onto The Bones." She hesitated. "Uh . . . well, I'm not sure. I just want to find out about such things." She paused. "Would you like the book? I don't want to delay your research."

He looked at her curiously, as if trying to understand her. "Oh, no, you keep the book for now. You seem to be getting just into it. I'm here for a while."

"A while?" May said, feeling a wave of nervousness pass over her. How could she perform her research in front of a real university student?

"Yes, I've come here especially to study the Pleiades." He smiled. "Do you know, May, that the other name for the Pleiades is Maia?"

"Maia? Why's that?"

"In the Greek myth, Maia was the eldest of the seven daughters of Atlas for whom the Pleiades are named. I want to see how those seven bright stars walk across the sky under the tent of a summer night." He paused, then added, "Maia was considered the most beautiful—perhaps because of the sparkle in her eyes. At least that is what makes her the most visible star in the constellation."

May felt a thrilling tingle go up her spine as he spoke but then felt immediately foolish. She had to leave before he noticed her blushing. "I really have to be going."

"Perhaps I could pick up the book from you next week?"

"I live on Egg Rock," she said hesitantly.

"The lighthouse?"

The way he said it sounded to May as if it were a million miles away.

"Yes," she replied.

"It's not a problem, I can get there. I've rented a small day sailer."

"Yes, yes, of course." Her pulse quickened at the thought of him coming to see her.

"Good-bye, then," he said, and smiled.

But as she walked away, she felt her stomach sink. Hugh would figure out a way to continue his research without going to all the trouble to sail to Egg Rock. He'd never come. He was just being polite. By tomorrow, he'd have forgotten all about her.

BELONGING

MAY COULD HEAR THE MUSIC from outside the Odd Fellows Hall. She hesitated and stood in the shadows of the big elm by the building. She could see the swirl of dancing figures inside through the tall windows. She had never been to a dance before, but she so wanted to be a part of something. She wanted to come home and have Zeeba see her cheeks pink from dancing. And for her father to say, "Who'd you dance with?"

I need to do this! she told herself firmly. *I need to be a normal girl, doing normal things.*

She walked quickly toward the front steps of the hall and pushed the door open. A twirling dancer brushed by her. Then Rudd appeared in front of her.

"I thought you weren't coming. Dance is half over. Where you been?" She recoiled at the slightly accusatory note in his voice. "Thought I was going to have to go out and hunt you down!" He laughed, and there again was the hard fierce light in his eyes that had unnerved May the first time they'd met. He must have sensed her discomfort, for immediately his eyes softened. He smiled, and a quick dimple appeared that she had never noticed before. In a flash, he seemed boyish and charming. "Come on, let's dance."

May smiled and forced the lingering thoughts of Hugh Fitzsimmons from her mind. Rudd was the handsomest young man in the hall. She should feel flattered by his attention.

"I'm not sure if I know how to dance," May replied. Zeeba had certainly never taught her.

"Yes, you do. It's easy. They're going to do a reel. Get into the line with the other girls and I'll be just across from you in the men's line."

"Hey, Rudd, I thought you were across from me! Aren't we partners for the Island Reel?" Susie Eaton said as Rudd slipped between Ralph Emery and Robert Cram.

"Rob's your partner this time round. May's mine," he answered.

May felt herself blush. The two short little words — *May's mine* — cut into her. What was it about the way Rudd Sawyer talked? It was as if there was a light and dark side to everything he said, a rough and a smooth. Another girl might be pleased as punch at the way he seemed to take an interest. And part of her was, too. She had to admit it. But at the same time there was a slight sense of danger. Still, danger was a welcome relief from the stultifying predictability of life in the lighthouse.

The fiddles struck up the tune and the dance began.

"Keep your eyes on me and you'll know just what to do, darlin'!"

Darlin'! No one had ever called May *darlin'* in her life. *Dear* or *de-ah* was the favored term of endearment of downeasters. But *darlin'* was a far cry from *dear*. It was something that younger men often called their sweethearts. May was hardly his sweetheart—yet. Nevertheless she felt a shiver of excitement.

She had scanned the room just before the music started. There were many familiar faces, schoolmates who were known sweethearts. They would get married very quickly upon high school graduation. Her eyes settled on Doug Hardy and his wife, Evie, who were sitting at the edge of the room. Her belly was sticking out to kingdom come with their seventh child. He was holding her hand. They had their heads tipped toward each other and were smiling and talking intimately. She was too pregnant to dance and he was too thoughtful to go out on the floor and leave her. But their enjoyment of a night out was obvious. They were having their own little dance in their own little world.

If May had an island sweetheart she could have that, too. She could get married out of high school. Have children. Not seven, but, say, two or three. That seemed enviable, but could it turn into the world of Gar and Zeeba? She looked up at Rudd. He was very handsome. He was a good fisherman. He didn't drink like a lot of them—at least as far as she knew. If he kept fishing he could have a little house in town like the other successful fishermen. She could be a fisherman's wife. That was as respectable as one could get on the coast, next to being a captain's wife. One thing for certain was that they would never move inland. Rudd would be as bound to the sea as she was. She looked over again at Evie and Doug Hardy. But could there ever be that ease, the trust between them, that seemed to radiate from this couple?

Rudd called her *darlin'* one more time. "See, darlin', you know how to dance," he said as they twirled around each other in the reel.

"Hush!" May felt herself turn scarlet. They stepped up to each other, then circled as the two lines of dancers began to weave together.

While the whirling dancers slid by her in what seemed an unending reel, she studied the rest of the people in the hall. The older folk sat on the sidelines in straight chairs, enjoying the music and the sight of the young people dancing. Many of them tapped their feet in time to the music, most likely remembering when they were young. Perhaps they had found their mates at a dance like this.

May had never waltzed before, but the three-quarter rhythm seemed made for her. She felt cradled by the music and yes, she had to admit, cradled by Rudd's arm around her waist. He was looking steadily down at her and the hard, bright glint in his eyes had melted away completely. She had always thought his eyes were a dark brown, nearly black, but now she was not so sure. They seemed lighter—not brown, more amber.

"You're a born dancer, May Plum."

She smiled. He pressed his hand into the small of her back and guided her around the dance floor as if he were sailing a skiff in a light breeze. She felt her skirt billow out. She felt happy and light and beautiful.

"You two look mighty smart together dancing," Phineas Heanssler said as he swept by with Susie Eaton.

"She's got a good helm on her, Phin!" Rudd said, and they all laughed, even May. Phineas Heanssler was the son of Raymond Heanssler, the best shipbuilder in Maine, and some said on the entire east coast. And there were those who said that the son Phineas was going to surpass him. To build a ship with a good helm took skill. It meant that the ship was balanced and didn't drag up to windward in a stiff breeze. Yes, May liked that Rudd had said she had a good helm.

Still, she couldn't quite banish Hugh from her thoughts. She wondered what he made of the Maury book. He was certainly familiar with it. But she shouldn't let herself think of him. He would never come to the island, and once the rich summer people arrived, he would be going to all their fancy parties and not dances at the Odd Fellows Hall. It would be champagne and debutantes from New York and Boston in elegant gowns. May had heard about these parties. She wondered if Hugh would be as shocked to discover those young ladies reading Maury's book as he had been when he'd found her.

She turned her thoughts back to the passages she had read earlier that evening, and the sense that she knew things about the sea he did not. How had it come to her? Because there was a part of her that belonged to the sea. *Yes, that's it!* she thought.

The press of people in the hall was almost too much. There was a sudden nearly stifling warmth. She tried to imagine Gar and Zeeba here over twenty years ago, dancing. Impossible! But Gar had said he had come to dances.

Suddenly all the faces seemed oddly strange to May. She felt a gulf opening up between herself and all the people at this dance. *I don't belong here.* She knew as surely as she had ever known anything that she was different, and she shuddered at the thought.

By the time they reached Rudd's skiff at the town dock, the fresh air had calmed May's nerves. "*Sea Pup?*" she said as she stepped aboard.

"Yeah, well, makes sense. The mother ship, Gus's, is *Sea Hound*," Rudd replied.

"Oh, yes, I forgot," she said quickly.

They had danced every dance until the band stopped playing. Now Rudd was sailing her back to Egg Rock. It was a lovely night. The moon was not quite full and slightly lopsided, with a hump swelling from one side that cast a silver path leading directly to Egg Rock.

"Nice night for a sail," Rudd said. "You going to be warm enough? You want to wear my coat?"

"Oh, I'm fine. I've got this shawl, and I don't often get cold."

Rudd said something under his breath that she could not quite understand, but it made her slightly nervous.

The wind was a favorable one, and they were soon skimming over the water. She peered out across the gleaming black expanse of Frenchman's Bay. The water was slightly wrinkled from the breeze, and the reflections of stars danced a skittish jig on the surface. She dipped her hand over the side.

"Whatcha doing, May?"

"Catching a star," she said, peering into the water.

"Me, too!" He leaned over and kissed her cheek. It was so quick she wasn't exactly sure what had happened until a second or two later.

"You kissed me!" It didn't feel bad, but May was not one for surprises. At least not this kind. It felt just a little bit as if he had sneaked up on her. Would Doug Hardy sneak up on Evie that way?

"I sure did. Want another one?"

She didn't say anything but pulled her shawl tighter around her and smiled into the thick wool. Zeeba was wrong. She wasn't unnatural. That kiss proved that she could be like the girls she saw at the dance. *Didn't it?*

Almost at the same moment she felt a presence surrounding the skiff, then something broke through the water. "Dolphins!" she cried. Two swam right up to the side of the skiff.

"Well, would ya look at that!" Rudd said. "I've never seen them do that—never so close! They'll come up to bigger boats to play off their bow waves. But *Sea Pup* isn't making much of a wave or a wake."

May's heart was racing. She turned around and kneeled so she could look at them eye to eye while resting her chin on the gunwales of the skiff. She put out her hand and stroked the head of the one closest to her. The dolphin rolled slightly to one side. Its dark eye had a joyous gleam. "You like that, don't you, de-ah," she whispered.

"May, what the devil you doing?" Rudd's voice was tense. She ignored him. "May?"

She felt the skiff head off course, but the dolphins followed.

Rudd headed a bit more off the wind. May heard a snap in the canvas. "Rudd, you're going to jibe this pup if you don't watch it."

"But, May, what are you doing?"

"I'm patting a dolphin," she said simply.

"It ain't normal." His hand jittered a bit on the tiller.

"Maybe I'm not normal," May whispered to the dolphin.

"What did you say?" Rudd asked.

May sighed. "Nothing."

He was silent for a while, then he leaned over and touched the locket that hung from her neck.

"Whatcha keep in that?" he asked.

She pulled back. "That's my business."

"Maybe someday it'll be mine. I got a picture of me you could put in it."

May didn't answer.

They were nearing the dock of Egg Rock. She gave the dolphins each one last pat. She spoke no words, for just her touch seemed to convey her meaning. *Again, soon!*

May was about to step onto the dock when Rudd yanked her down onto the seat of the boat and pulled her toward his chest. He kissed her hard on the mouth. It wasn't a nice kiss, but wet and sloppy. He crushed her against him, but she pushed back and he almost fell overboard. She reached for her bag with the chimney and the book and jumped straight onto the dock, leaving the skiff rocking.

"What's wrong with you, girl?" Rudd spat. "I mean,

you almost miss a dance to read in the library and then pass up a chance to kiss me?"

"I've got a good helm, remember?"

In that instant the dreams she had toyed with at the dance, of a life of sweet intimacy with a fisherman husband and their children, dissolved like shreds of fog in a brightening day. It suddenly seemed every bit as stifling as living in the lighthouse, swapping one kind of imprisonment for another. She had played with the idea as a child might play with a new doll for a while, and then seeing in those eyes a terrible emptiness, tossed the doll aside.

FIRST SELF

MAY COULD NOT SLEEP. Why had Rudd said that she wasn't normal when she had reached over the side of the skiff to stroke the dolphin? She thought of those nice women. Of Evie Hardy, expecting her seventh child. Of Susie Eaton. And then she remembered how hard it struck her that she might be different — not just being from far away but separate from the placid life of the village women. *"It ain't normal!"* Rudd's words reverberated in her ears. She knew she had to go upstairs and take the Saint Anthony key and open the small door, then lift the lid on that chestful of darkness. She had to understand what made her different.

Her hands were trembling as she unlocked the

small door in the watch room. The lantern cast some light, but it did not quite reach into the closet, and the sea chest was steeped in shadows. She lifted the lid, and before she could even touch the blanket, that scent from the heart of the sea rolled out, engulfing her. She closed her eyes for a moment and then bent over the edge of the chest. Something sparkled in the frayed threads of the old blanket. It was not the glimmer of her hair. *What in the world?*

Scattered into the weave of the blanket and on the bottom of the chest were tiny oval crystals, almost teardrop in shape. They shimmered with a pale iridescence that seemed to glow more intensely with the passing seconds. She picked one up on the tip of her finger and looked at it. A rush of joy surged through her. *This, too, is part of me!*

In that moment she knew she would never be sitting with her hands folded placidly over a belly with child, a woman married to a fisherman, anchored in a town on an island. She knew she was from very far away. She opened her locket and put several of the small ovals into it. Then once again she took a pin from her hair and picked out the red filament of her baby hair and added it to the locket. As soon as she closed the locket's clasp, the most amazing calm crept through her.

Rudd's angry words faded away, replaced by another sound—the crash of waves. Except it wasn't coming from outside the lighthouse. It seemed to flow from the locket. The sea was calling.

She experienced a feeling of illumination, as if she had absorbed the iridescence of those teardrop-shaped crystals she had tucked in the locket. A glow had been kindled deep within her. She rose up and carefully closed the lid of the chest. And as if in a waking sleep, she locked the door of the small closet, replaced the key behind the carved figure of Saint Anthony, and began to walk down the stairs. She could hear her father's snoring as she slipped out the front door, and quiet as a ghost, made her way past Bells Two, as they called this cow, the daughter of the original Bells. The cow might have blinked as she saw a radiant wake stream out behind May like a jeweled mist. May, the girl who milked her every morning! But cows do not wonder, and the beast remained dumb and moo-less.

May made her way to the cliffs. They were not high cliffs, but she knew that beneath them the water was deep. She dropped her shawl, removed the calico jacket, stepped out of her skirt, and stood in her blouse and muslin petticoat. She took off her shoes and stockings. There was a chill in the air, but she didn't seem to feel the cold at all. As she stood with her toes curled over the very edge of the cliff, she looked down into the swirling waters below. She was suspended between the two oceans, the invisible one of air and the visible one of water.

She took a deep breath, her last for now from that invisible world, and touched the locket at her throat. If she had any doubts or fears, they vanished at that instant. A world awaited her and she belonged to it. She dove, and for a second or maybe two, she was suspended.

There seemed to be no impact. She sliced through the water neatly, cradled by the swirling currents. Streams of bubbles flowed about her, and she spread out her hands toward them. *I am catching stars*. She laughed and was startled to see that two large bubbles streamed from her mouth, yet she seemed to be breathing fine. She was not aware of swallowing any water at all. She drew her arms back toward her body and was surprised by how strongly she thrust forward in the water. *I CAN SWIM! I CAN SWIM! I AM SWIMMING!*

The ocean eddying through her mind was no longer a dream. It was real. She had crossed a border from one world into another. The colorful underwater tapestry was even more brilliant than she had imagined. The seaweed, which at low tide lay on the rocks in ugly tangled clumps that some called witch's hair, streamed like banners of amber lightning through the deep water. Moonlight and star shine fell into the depths, trimming the liquid night with a filigree of trembling lace.

Her bursts of speed amazed her. She soon was aware that all this speed was not coming from her arms but . . . her legs? She gave a powerful kick and found herself racing to the surface, breaking through it into a high arcing leap. The moon and the stars that had quivered in the sea now seemed rock solid and anchored to the sky. *Good lord, am I flying to heaven? A* slight tingling radiated just beneath her skin, and she was struck by the sense that her legs were no longer legs but had become a tail—glistening and beautiful.

When she plunged back into the water she rolled onto her back and lifted her tail above the water's surface, looking at it with amazement. She touched the locket around her neck; the iridescent sparkles that gilded her tail were identical to the flattened crystal ovals she had picked from the frayed blanket. She had lost her legs, and yet she had become whole.

A moment later the two dolphins she had seen with Rudd swam up to her. They greeted her in a watery language that had no words, but that May understood immediately. It was as if she had discovered a different order of thinking, a new kind of cognition. She heard more clearly, felt every feathery current of the sea, and now seemed to be able to communicate without words. She swam far out with the dolphins, beyond The Bones to the rocks that were marked on the charts as Simon's Ledge. They were several miles offshore, but May and the dolphins had reached their destination in a short time. And when they arrived, she knew almost instantly why the dolphins had brought her to these ledges. This was where she had left the sea, from the time she was an infant. This was where Edgar Plum had found her, in that sea chest. She looked at the two dolphins and stroked their heads.

The dolphins had found her where two minor gyres intersected. Unsure how long the chest would last, they drove her toward the nearest fishing boat they could find. But May felt for sure that there were others out there someplace. There were three mermaids carved on the chest. "They are my kin," she whispered to herself, but this the dolphins did not understand.

Snow had started to fall, big fluffy flakes descending quietly from the dark bowl of the starry night. An April fools' joke, for she realized that this was the first of April. But snow along the coast of Maine in April was no surprise. What surprised May was that she still did not feel cold, not even cool. The irksome variations in temperature that she had felt on land, which would make her run for a shawl or chafe against a high-collared dress in the heat of summer, no longer seemed to affect her. It suddenly struck her that for all these years, she had been a rather clumsy visitor on land. She flinched as the very thought sent a momentary pain shooting through her. How could she return to that life? Pretending to be something she was not, surrounded by people who could never understand?

May was not sure how long she had been swimming. The darkness had begun to fray until the sky looked worn, the thin light of dawn seeping into the new day. But she could not tear herself away and kept swimming until the last star faded into the final remnants of the night. There was a glimmering of pink, then gold on the horizon. The snow had stopped and there was a crispness in the air as she watched the sun rise in the east. And with this dawn, clarity of thought came to her as well. *My kin might be on land still—like myself—or they might have died.* But the second part of that thought was unendurable. She knew they were still somewhere out there, and so she returned to land.

THE HALF OF IT

THE SHEETS FELT ODD and the mattress lumpy, but hadn't they always been that way? May wondered as she awakened after a brief hour's sleep. It was the absence of movement that struck her first—that billowing motion that had enveloped her all while she was in the sea; that absence as well as an odd sense of disconnection. When she had been swimming she felt fused with life, with Earth. There was a vital correspondence with all living things as if she were plumbing the most basic elements from which life arose. But she had left that liquid essence behind, and now the sheets seemed to scratch, the mattress felt lumpy, and just then there was that familiar caw.

"May! May!" Zeeba's voice outside her bedroom splintered the air.

"What?"

"Would you mind explaining something to me, young lady?"

Young lady! May winced. She felt like calling back, "What do you want, old lady?"

Zeeba was standing just outside her door and shoved it open now. "What in tarnation is that flying on the clothesline?"

May looked out the window from her bedroom. She began to laugh. Her wet petticoat had frozen solid and was now dancing in a stiff breeze. Luckily her tail had quickly dissolved into two very human legs when she had returned from her miraculous awakening. She had peeled off the wet petticoat, put on her skirt, blouse, and calico jacket, and proceeded to hang the petticoat on the clothesline. It wasn't wash day, and usually when only one garment had to be washed in cold weather, they hung it up to dry inside near the wood-burning stove. But May had wanted to be as quiet as possible when she returned to the house a few hours before and hadn't thought twice about hanging it out-side. She certainly didn't want anyone finding salt-water stains on the wood floor.

"I just rinsed it last night when I came back from the dance and hung it out to dry, Zeeba."

"Hrrumph!" was the only utterance she heard as Zeeba turned away and walked back to the kitchen.

May couldn't resist. "You must be feeling better. You're up earlier than I am."

The creak of the floorboards stopped. She could imagine Hepzibah fuming now. To comment posi-tively on Hepzibah's health was to enter dangerous territory. Hepzibah did not take kindly to any sort of comments on the improvement of her health by anyone who was not a physician. She didn't even like doctors to express too much hope. She preferred that they remain confounded or at least perplexed.

May got up, dressed, and went about her chores as she usually did, but she was suddenly aware of how awkward everything felt, from the ground under the milking stool as she sat to milk Bells Two to the stairs winding up to the lantern room when she went to dust the lenses. She wondered if she looked odd doing these tasks. Did she walk funny? She felt very peculiar. There was that expression "like a fish out of water"—was that what she now appeared to be?

When May had completed her chores, she knew she should go back downstairs, join her father for a mug of tea, and go over the shipping news, the accounts that listed any merchant vessels that might be plying the regular routes from Halifax to Boston or the reverse. But she was hesitant. Would he find a change in her? Were there any telltale signs of what had happened the previous night? When he had found her in that sea chest as an infant, did she have—she smiled softly to herself—a tail? Two days before, she would have been staggered and embarrassed if such a thought had crossed her mind, but now she wanted desperately to ask him—*Did I have a tail?* There were, after all, those glistening little ovals that she now knew were scales in the chest. She took a deep breath and started down the stairs.

She slid her eyes cautiously toward the pine table

where Gar was sitting. He was deeply engrossed in the shipping news and did not look up. But she did observe that her father seemed better than he had in weeks and had even put on his uniform. He was now freshly shaved, wearing his vest, jacket, and cap as he sat at the table, reading. He looked ready for light-house business.

"Pa, is it time already for another inspection?"

"No, de-ah, not for another month." He looked up at her brightly, and she felt color rise in her cheeks. "They never get up here until first week of May. But you've been doing more than your share of the work these last weeks. My hip hardly gives me a twinge. So I'll be helping out more. And I never seen you look prettier than this morning." Something lurched in her stomach. "Dancing agrees with you."

Relief swept through her, and it was all she could do to refrain from saying, "Not dancing, Pa, swimming."

"Now, tomorrow," her father continued, "I'm going to take you in on the skiff. I want you to be able to finish up school this term."

"Oh!" she exclaimed nervously. Did this mean he was thinking about sending her inland when she finished her schooling? Had he picked up on something and wanted to get her as far away from the sea as possible? If Gar was trying to separate her from the sea, she would have to flee—flee to her true home and find her true kin.

"Pa, don't misunderstand, I want to go back to school, but I really don't want to go to Augusta or Bridgeton when I graduate."

"Well, that's not why I want you to go to school. You need to be with young folk—like you were at the dance."

A sigh issued forth from the corner of the kitchen where Hepzibah was rattling a spoon noisily in a glass of one of her tonics.

"Yes, that would be nice. And, Pa, maybe I could help Miss Lowe at the library right in Bar Harbor. I mean, that would be good, wouldn't it? I'm sure she needs help. And it wouldn't be so far away, you know."

"Well, it's a tiny library—not like in Augusta. So

I'm not sure how much help she would need," her father replied.

May was now desperate to change the subject. "Funny about that snow. Not a flake of it stuck. Just April fools', I guess."

"What snow?" Edgar Plum asked.

"Late last night, almost at dawn. It snowed . . . didn't it?" May asked nervously.

"You were up?"

"No, no," she paused. "I must have dreamed it."

The rattling of the spoon in the glass stopped. Hepzibah turned around slowly and fixed her eyes on May. "You must have dreamed it because I was up. I got one of those terrible back cramps. The only way to get rid of it is to wrap a hot brick, tuck it behind my back, and sit in that chair. I didn't see no snow."

"You were up?" May said weakly.

"Certainly was."

Hepzibah was up and hadn't caught her coming back into the house? She rarely came into May's tiny little bedroom on the landing a quarter way up the tower. But nonetheless May could have been caught returning. She must be careful when she went out again, which she planned to do as soon as possible.

For May had formed a larger plan and knew that the time was approaching for a very long swim. A swim to find the *Resolute*. She had to figure out where in the vast Atlantic the bones of that ship lay. She needed to study the tracks of the sea, learn about them through Maury's wind-and-current studies, and through swimming herself. She would have to build up her own strength, her stamina. But there was something else beyond her own abilities that was crucial for this swim. It was as if she were waiting for someone to go with her, accompany her. She did not want to go alone.

After finishing her tea she returned to the watch room of the lighthouse and read Matthew Fontaine Maury. The book that had seemed so impenetrable to her the day before, she now read with a new understanding. Maury only wrote about the currents of wind and sea, but she had swum them. He had only thought about the tug of the opposing gyres and eddies off the New England coast, but she had felt them. He had his theories based on a combination of Scripture and mathematics, but she had been born to them. He had been a lieutenant in the navy, but she was a daughter of the sea, and she was determined to find her kin. *Oh, Mr. Maury,* she thought. *You don't know the half of it!*

THE BONES

EVERY NIGHT FOR THE NEXT WEEK, May slipped out to the sea. Each time she slid into the water she was overwhelmed by a powerful sense of belonging, finally being at home. She had no fears whatsoever. She had seen sharks, but they seemed to avoid her. She had become familiar with the grinding noise of the steamboat engines that brought people up from Boston to Bar Harbor and the slicing sound of a sailing schooner's keel as it passed through the water. It did not take her long to learn the navigation routes of the larger vessels in order to avoid them. On one of her first nights, she had nearly ensnared herself in a herring weir. Ever since, she'd kept a keen lookout for the bobbing buoys to which the vast nets were attached. She swam every current between Egg Rock and Eastport and then down to Cape Rosier. These were distances of forty miles or more, but she could cover them in a night of swimming, especially if she took advantage of the tides and the normal currents.

On the fifth night after she had crossed over she became aware of a slightly altered quality in the water on either side of her. It was as if there were pockets of air, voids in the water. At first she thought they were large bubbles of some sort, but they had no contours. She was most acutely aware of these spaces that flanked her body when she swam, but she had begun to sense them on land as well. She longed for these voids to be filled, to reveal themselves.

If she understood the tracks of the sea, she might be able to determine where the *Resolute*'s wreckage could be found, even fifteen years after it went down. Had there been another sea chest? Three mermaids were carved on the one that Gar had pulled from the sea. Could that mean that there were two others beside herself? That she had sisters?

There was one place her swimming had not yet taken her: The Bones, where the schooner had wrecked. She was afraid to go there, afraid of what she might see—dead men, their unseeing eyes staring dumbly into a watery eternity, their bones. Perhaps fish had scavenged their flesh. The idea was unnerving. And yet she knew that she must dive this wreck. She needed to understand how the currents might have disturbed it; how the fractured timbers from the ship could have been swirled away.

One evening, a week after her transformation, May determined she would go. As she was approaching The Bones, she could see that rigging lines were still tangled around some of the rocks. She gasped when she saw a baby seal thrashing about in an eddy. He had been snagged by rigging and was now crying, his mother barking desperately.

She swam close to the seal pup. His eyes were rolled back in his head. He was so exhausted when she approached that he didn't even put up a fight when she tried to lift his snagged flipper. She treaded water with her tail, and sang a water song that seemed to come to her while stroking the pup's head:

"Hssshong goorahn lathem
Prishamg lohrrinn nasquit
Amara Blarring Blarrin"

It was the watery language that she seemed to know without even realizing that she knew it. The words seemed to hearken to an old memory from the very beginning of her life, and she felt those spaces on either side of her begin to tremble. The seal pup grew calm, and May was able to free his flipper so he could swim back to his mother, who greeted him with yips and whimpers of relief. The mother seal tossed May a fish, but May was not hungry. Still she felt it wouldn't be right to refuse it. She took a bite and giggled when she realized she was actually eating raw fish. It didn't taste bad at all. Very fresh, but not bloody like rare meat.

On her first dive down to the wreck she spotted the rudder stuck firmly into the sea bottom. But she still couldn't see the hull, and the churning water kicked up screens of sand and mud. The currents were confused here, and there were more eddies than May could count. But she was patient. She anchored herself beside the rudder and decided to wait and watch. She had found that she could stay underwater for great lengths of time and only needed to surface for a few quick gulps of air. May knew that if she waited long enough, she would find a pattern to the seemingly confused currents.

A large school of smelt arrived on the back eddy of one current she had been watching. Almost immediately she noticed them caught by another, stronger current that sucked them straight out from The Bones. She swam in that direction.

It wasn't long before she saw the hull of the ship rearing from the seafloor. It was half the hull, for as she recalled it had split in two just before it was raked off The Bones. The currents swirled in a counterclockwise direction, so the rest of the ship and its debris might have been carried south and west from this point. Had this happened to the *Resolute* as well? The letter mentioned a lifeboat being found south of Martha's Vineyard. It was as if the ships were caught in a cross fire of wind and currents and their parts were strewn all over the ocean floor.

But she soon spied the other half, the bow, not far from the aft part of the schooner. The bow was destroyed, but the aft section was amazingly intact. It sat up on the remnants of its keel and looked ready to resume life at sea. There were even portholes still intact. Slowly May approached the round windows. It was a miracle that the glass had not been smashed to smithereens. She was frightened to look in. What if there was a dead man? The captain had never been found. Suppose he was still sitting at his navigation desk? She swam closer, then pressed her nose to the glass. No dead man, but she almost swallowed a mouthful of water and choked. For what stared back at her was a pale face. Was it a specter? She raised her hand, and the specter did as well. She waved and then smiled. She knew that this was her reflection, and yet with the slight distortion caused by the water, she could imagine another being almost identical to herself. Once again she felt the tingle in those empty spaces and the song she had sung to the seal pup filled her head once more. She pressed her mouth to the glass and whispered, "Someone sang us the song. Someone really did."

The following morning, after she had finished her chores, May went down to the beach to gaze out to sea. She was thinking about the reflection in the porthole. Water, she knew, distorted light, bent it. This was not called *reflection*, but *refraction*. If she gave it time, she might better understand those mysterious shapes that seemed to swim beside her. She was thinking about all of this when she caught sight of a small day sailer approaching Egg Rock. The lines of the boat were unmistakable. It was a Phineas Heanssler craft. It must be Hugh—Hugh Fitzsimmons! He was actually coming for the book. She could not quite believe it. She had tried to banish any thought of him since the dance. But she looked out now and saw that sail with a bellyful of wind pulling him toward Egg Rock. Then it dawned on her: She had to get the book before he walked up to the lighthouse. There was no way she would let him inside. Zeeba was especially cranky today. And what would she think of a college boy from away? It would be like mixing oil and water.

May took off and raced up to the path. She must get the book before he got to the dock. A few minutes later she was on the ramp of the dock, panting slightly, with the book in hand.

"Hello!" she called when he was a few yards from the dock's float. He let the sails flap as the boat coasted in.

"Hello, May. Great day for a sail." He was wearing a broad-brimmed hat—a summer-folk hat—that cast a slanting shadow across his face. "Can you catch my line?"

He tossed her the painter. She jumped up, still with the book in one hand, and caught the tail end midair. "Good aim," she said.

"Good catch." Even through the shadow she saw the flash of his smile.

"I'd invite you up to the house but my mother's not very well today. But we can walk around the island. It's not very big."

"That would be lovely."

"Here's the book," she said, extending her arm. She did not look at him directly. She was unsure what to say next—how to continue the conversation.

"You don't need it anymore, May? You're sure?"

"Well, I might need it again sometime. But no, really, you take it for now."

He tucked it into a satchel and then climbed onto the float. "This island is beautiful. Not a tree on it, but a lovely place."

"There was a tree once—once upon a time."

"You make it sound like a fairy tale."

"Sometimes I think it was. The tree came and went long before my time." She inhaled sharply. "It's a hard place to live and grow." He looked at her and seemed about to say something, and then—she saw it clearly in his eyes—he decided not to.

"Where do you come from?" May asked.

"Rhode Island, but I spent a lot of time in Washington, DC, growing up."

"Why?"

"Why what?"

"How can you be from Rhode Island but grow up in another place? It's different here, I guess."

"Oh, it was my father's job. He was a congressman back then."

"You mean in the United States Congress?" May's eyes opened wide.

"Yes."

"You said 'back then.' What does he do now?"

"Well, now he's a senator, actually."

May was almost speechless. The very air seemed to beg the question. *What in the world are you doing here on Egg Rock?* The words pounded in her head.

They walked around to the east-facing beach, just beneath the cliff she always dove from. The wind had died, and the water stretched out before them like a metallic sheet. It was an unusually warm day for this time of year.

"You ever go swimming here?" Hugh asked.

It was as if she had been punched squarely in the guts. "Never!" she answered quickly, and there must have been a sharpness in her voice, for Hugh turned to look at her, a flicker of surprise in his eyes.

"The currents, I suppose?" he replied. "But not even wading?"

"Not even wading," she said softly. "What are you doing?"

He laughed and bent over and began to unlace his shoes. "I'm going wading. Come on, join me."

"No, I'd rather not." She shut her eyes tight. She saw her feet—the glistening scales melting out from beneath her skin. Her toes gradually fusing together . . . *I am a freak!* And she felt the first tiny fissure cracking in her heart when she looked down at his tousled head as he peeled off his socks. His feet were slender and white. He rolled up the cuffs of his pants. His calves were strong.

When he looked at her over his shoulder his gray

eyes twinkled. "You're absolutely sure you don't want to go wading?"

No! No! I'm not sure at all. I'm not sure of anything! she wanted to scream. But instead she merely nodded and replied in a low voice, "I'm sure."

LUCKY

MAY WAS WALKING BACK FROM SCHOOL. She had not seen Hugh since the day he had come to pick up the book. But since then he had occupied her thoughts completely.

May had replayed their walk on the beach in her mind a hundred times. There were moments when she thought that he had looked at her as if he was interested in her. When she had said that Egg Rock was a hard place in which to live and grow, it seemed that he had wanted to ask her more but had stopped himself. Was this the detached curiosity of a scientist or something else? It was neither, she thought. *He is the son of a senator. I'm not his kind. Not anyone's kind!*

The image of him removing his shoes and socks was burnished in her mind. She was sure he thought her behavior odd, but that was nothing compared to what he would have thought of her feet if her toes began to web and her skin broke out in its shimmering rash of scales. Before that day she had considered her scales beautiful, but now they felt like a sickness or an allergy. Until Hugh had shown up at Egg Rock, her life since her transformation had arranged itself into two neatly organized existences. At night she crossed a border into one world. By dawn she was back—the slightly awkward tourist in the other world. She thought that she might learn how to balance the two. But since that day on the beach, she realized that it was not likely. The freedom she had reveled in had darkened.

She was always on the lookout for Hugh. He did not seem to be around the village, and when she had asked at the library two days ago, Miss Lowe had said that he had to go back to Boston for a "family reason." The two words sent a shudder through May. *Of course, he has family.* Why had she never thought of that before? Something wilted in her as the unspeakable thought flooded through her. Hugh Fitzsimmons had a proper Rhode Island family. She was only a downeast island girl with no family, and only part human. *Which part*, she wondered. *Where does my humanity begin and where does it end?*

When May went to school, which she did much more regularly these days, she was caught between the hope and despair of seeing him. So far she had not, and although she always felt slightly deflated, she knew it was for the best.

School seemed rather dull to her since she had returned. Two older girls had dropped out to marry. She was now the oldest student in the small clapboard building on East Street, the only sophomore. Miss Gilbert, the teacher, had her hands full with some rowdy eleven-year-old boys, and May seemed to spend most of her time helping eighth graders learn about common denominators. Her swim to the

Josiah B. Harwood made it clear that she needed to learn about something called vector diagrams, which showed the motion of an object if it was influenced by forces in more than one direction. Forces like wind and current and objects like the broken hull of the *Josiah B. Harwood* and the spars of the *Resolute*. If she could learn this kind of math, she might be able to calculate where the main part of the wreck of the *Resolute* lay in this vast ocean. But poor Miss Gilbert just didn't have the time. And good lord, May was sick of teaching kids about common denominators. Percentiles, too! Leon Beal could not for the life of him understand that percentiles were just another way of expressing fractions. And his nose was perpetually snotty, dripping all over his math papers.

May was walking through town toward the wharf because Cletus Weed, the mail boat captain, had said he could drop her off and spare her father the trip.

"A penny for your thoughts, MayPlum."

It sounded like one word to her, the way Rudd said her name. Since she had started going to school more regularly, he often caught up with her before she hopped on the mail boat to go back to Egg Rock. He was more deferential, that was for sure. But on the other hand the glint in his eyes had hardened and was no longer simply a flirtatious gleam but one of suspicion. May felt she had to move carefully, and it was perhaps best to keep things light. "Oh, I wouldn't know where to begin with such penny thoughts." *With Leon Beal's snot, perhaps?*

"At the beginning, maybe."

But there was no beginning, really, or at least not one beginning. Since her dive to the *Josiah B. Harwood*, her head had been filled with all sorts of thoughts concerning drift and currents and winds as she tried to calculate where the *Resolute* might be. She was now more certain than ever that the ship had been her birthplace.

After her initial forays into the study of vector diagrams with a book she had found in the library, it was as if she had opened a mathematical can of worms. She had to learn some trigonometry, too, as it would help her pinpoint the location of the wreck. Dr. Holmes had come into the library just that afternoon and sat with her for forty-five minutes to try to teach her some of the very basic formulas, which focused on measuring the surfaces of spheres. This in theory should help her figure out where the wreckage of the *Resolute* might have drifted.

Should she start speaking in formulas to Rudd? The angle of addition—sine A over sine a = sine B over sine b = sine C over sine c? She had looked at countless charts and maps. She had now reached the conclusion that the wreck of the *Resolute* was either on the edge of Georges Bank or Nantucket Shoals, or possibly the Gulf Stream.

Miss Lowe had even helped her look for old newspapers and had written to the Augusta library. She turned to Rudd. He was easy to fool.

"Oh, I guess I was just dreaming," she said, and smiled.

"Dreaming of what?" he asked.

Again she noticed that glint of suspicion. He had no right to ask her what she was dreaming. She resented it, just like when he had asked her about the locket. But she had vowed to keep the conversation light. She must look as if she were just another high school girl thinking about the next dance, a new dress, a new hairstyle. But it wasn't that easy with Rudd. He might not be smart in the way Hugh was—book smart—but he was sly. She often thought that Rudd might perceive some change in her long before Hugh ever could. For Rudd knew the sea and he knew fish. The thought was alarming. She had heard him on the wharf, bragging about how he could sense where the cod runs would be or the alewife schooling, and May often felt as if he were looking at her. Rudd Sawyer was gaining a reputation as one of the best offshore fishermen on Mount Desert. He had a knack for setting weirs where the biggest schools of young cod and striped bass swam. Then offshore they said he just seemed to have an uncanny sense for where the sword and big cod went for their prey—hake, squid, bluefish. He was making a lot of money and was said to have the largest share of the catch other than Gus Bridges, captain of the *Sea Hound.*

She had to act polite. Striking the right tone was going to be hard. She didn't want to sound flirtatious but not outright rude. "Now, Rudd Sawyer, a girl never tells her dreams lest they won't come true." She forced a smile. "But actually I was just thinking about some mathematics problems that Doctor Holmes was helping me with when I was at the library." She looked down at the papers she was carrying in a folder.

"Mathematics—now, why does a girl need to know mathematics?"

"Why does a boy need to know it?" she answered tartly. *Watch it, May,* she warned herself.

"How's your fishing?" she asked before he had the chance to respond.

This was not a question she especially wanted to ask, but she needed to appear strong, fearless. He wanted to brag to her? Let him brag. She'd play her part, even if it meant she had to seem flirtatious. She had a sense that Rudd was one of those people who grew more aggressive the harder he was pushed.

"Good! Good!" he replied. "You know what?"

"What?" She tipped her head and smiled. Her green eyes twinkled.

"I tell you what, MayPlum, I earned more than any other fisherman in Bar Harbor save Captain Gus. How about that? Going to start building me a house— right out on the point toward Otter Creek."

"Oh, that's a beautiful place. I'm surprised the rich summer folk haven't bought up that piece."

"They ain't going to. I already put down five hundred dollars on it."

"Five hundred dollars!" May blinked and shook her head in disbelief. "Why, I never." It was an unimaginable sum to May.

He stepped up and chucked her under the chin. She recoiled at his touch.

"You see, May, I'm getting me a nest egg. I'm not going to drink it away like half these fellows. I have plans."

"Plans." May repeated the word softly.

"Come down to the fish wharf and see the boat and our catch. We just brought it in."

She didn't want to, but it was on her way, and she sensed it was best to humor him.

She saw the *Sea Hound* at the end of the wharf, bobbing in the water by the dock. Two men were putting cod into barrels underneath a line on which the glistening silver-blue bodies of swordfish hung. The fish twirled softly in the spring breeze. She felt a pang deep inside her as she looked at the *Sea Hound*. This was the way it was, she knew. Men fished here. It was their livelihood. She ate fish five out of seven days of the week. But there was something unsettling seeing these magnificent swordfish dangling by their tails, their eyes clouded in death, their scales that in the water ranged from silver to gray to blue with hints of bronze and even purple now dull and lusterless. Only the night before, she had swum through a school of swordfish, perhaps one hundred or more. She was larger. They made way for her, parting slightly, never even grazing her with their swords. She had traveled with them for the better part of an hour, their silvery blue radiance folding around her as she swam.

"How—how do you get them?"

"Harpoon. Come on board. Meet Lucky."

"Who's Lucky?" she asked as he helped her onto the deck of the *Sea Hound*.

Rudd reached up to where a number of harpoons were hanging on a frame at the stern along with gutting knives and the curved sawtoothed blades for scraping scales. "This is Lucky," he said, taking down a harpoon. The shaft was almost ten feet long and terminated in a lethal-looking dart with a barb. "You see?" Rudd's finger traced the point. "It's so sharp, it can go through bone. But the barb sets it. So the fish can't get away."

"Showing off, are you?" A man with a bushy iron-gray beard had walked up to where they stood.

"Hello, Captain. This here's May Plum, Gar Plum's daughter. From the lighthouse."

"Hello, Miss Plum. So Rudd here is showing off. Well, I guess he has cause. Nine out of those fifteen swordfish hanging up there got cozy with his harpoon. Feel like going back to lobstering, Rudd?" The captain winked at May.

"Don't be a fool! That ain't fishing, Captain Gus. That's like babysitting or watching grass grow. This is hunting. Here, May, want to hold the harpoon?"

"No, no thanks. I better be going."

Before he could say anything more May jumped up onto the pier.

"Well, she's a quick little thing, Rudd! Don't know how you'll catch her." Rudd just laughed and jumped up after her.

"Oh, I'm quick, too. So I'll see you at the apple blossom dance, MayPlum?"

Over his shoulders she could see the swordfish twisting on their hooks. *Dead*, she thought. Had she ever seen anything that looked more dead?

"When's that?" she asked.

"When the apple blossoms come out. End of second week of June."

"Uh . . . I don't know . . . maybe." It was hard for May to imagine a dance when she saw the lovely dead fish dangling from a line.

"Oh, my!" Captain Gus turned from the rope he

had been splicing and grinned at her. "She playing you, Rudd?"

Rudd dipped his chin into his collar and seemed to chuckle at some private joke, then shook his head. "No, no one plays me, Gus." He gave May what appeared to be a playful shove on the shoulder, but it was just enough to set her slightly off balance. The folder with the papers slipped, catching in a sudden gust of wind and lazily drifting toward the water.

"Oh, no!" May cried. "My proofs!"

Then quicker than when she had jumped up onto the pier, she leaped down to the deck of the *Sea Hound* again, grabbed Lucky, and raced to the stern platform.

"What the hell are you doing, girl?" Rudd yelled.

"Hey!" Captain Gus laughed. "I'd say that girl has a way with a harpoon. Look at her fetching those papers up now!" May was dipping the harpoon into the water and had managed to get the ones closest to the hull of the boat.

Rudd laughed, too, then in a flat voice said, "Guess she'll have to go swimming for the rest." May felt the blood drain from her face and swayed. She grabbed for the line of the riding sail on the stern to steady herself. *Does he know?* She slid her eyes toward him. She had expected to see him laughing at her, thinking this was some great joke. But he wasn't laughing at all. He was watching her carefully. His eyes reminded her of sharks' eyes—blank, almost dead, but seeing everything.

16

WAITING

SHE SAW IT GLINTING AND SHARP, a spike through
the deep gray of the offshore night water. The sky
was gray as well, slung low and heavy. It seemed to
press down on the sea until the two oceans, the visible and the invisible, were fused. It had been raining
when she slipped out. There was no moon, no light
to reflect, yet this glinting spike stabbed the murky
netherworld. Just ahead a trickle of blood threaded
through the grayness. A beautiful dying swordfish!
The spike had found its mark! Suddenly there were
scores of blades, spikes, and harpoons. She swam
wildly through a daggered forest. But one harpoon
grazed her tail. It seemed to have a life of its own
and it kept following her. The dart, polished to a

blazing silver, enveloped her in a blinding light. *"So sharp . . . can go through bone."* Lucky! It's Lucky!

I am going to die.

"No, no, MayPlum, just getting cozy—that's all."

May sat straight up in bed. She was sweating—sweating pure salt. "A dream, just a dream," she whispered. She looked out the window. It was still raining as it had been when she went out swimming six hours before. She had come back just an hour ago. But this dream was so real. She shivered and wrapped her arms tightly around her shoulders. She never felt cold from swimming. It was the dream that made her cold, not the sea.

Since her transformation, May seemed to need much less sleep. She could only surmise that this was the mer part of her. She had never seen a sea creature sleeping. When she did sleep, her dreams were intensely vivid. It was not just the colors of the sea that had seeped into the deepest parts of her being but its rhythms as well. This dream, however, had a different kind of intensity. There was a forceful-ness, a terrible violence. It was as if the harpoon had an intelligence, a mind of its own.

"You're a fool, May Plum," she said hoarsely. It was a dream, nothing more! She held herself tighter, but it was as if she were trying to embrace more than just herself. The twin voids, the spaces that pressed against her—had they been with her in her dream? She recalled the strange reflection in the porthole of the *Josiah B. Harwood.*

She was waiting. Waiting for the others, waiting for her two mer sisters, and when she found them they would go together. With them at her side, she could swim through a sea bristling with harpoons and sliced by the long daggers of her nightmare.

AVALONIA

FAR, FAR ACROSS THE ATLANTIC an island rises green from the sea. It is Barra Head, the southernmost of the islands known as the Outer Hebrides. It is girded by rough gray rocks from a time before time when two huge continents were one. Gradually an ocean formed and though it was only water, like the sharp edge of an anvil, the Atlantic chiseled the continents apart. They drifted their separate ways, at first just by inches but then by miles. The only evidence of their former union were the rocks embedded with similar fossils from their shared time as one continent. But sometimes these rocks were broken in two and were never to be matched to make a whole, like a jigsaw puzzle left half done. Small islands trailed in the wakes of both continents. Barra Head was one of these islands, washed by the calmer waters of a strait called the Little Minch, which separated the Outer Hebrides from the large Isle of Skye, just off the Scottish coast.

Round the tip of the island was a cave, the home of a mer woman. She was regarded as a hermit by the few inhabitants of the island—half a dozen crofting families who raised barley, potatoes, oats, and turnips and kept flocks of sheep. The folk of the island did not know that Avalonia, or Ava as she was known, was mer. To them she appeared not young, nor really old, but extremely beautiful, her deep auburn hair run through with threads of silver. Despite her beauty, men did not bother her. They seemed to sense a peculiar strength in her that perhaps they found threatening, but mostly they thought of her as different.

No one knew that she led a divided life, a secret life as a creature who swam far out into the sea, whose legs dissolved into a great and powerful tail every time she dove into the water. Her closest companions were seals. They sometimes swam to her cave, and when she went abroad they sought her company as a swimming companion, for she was gentle with their pups, and very playful. So it did not surprise her to look up and find a seal mother and young pup swimming toward her cave.

The seals clambered up on the small beach. They loved to come right into her cave. They would peer about in wonder at the wreaths she had made from seashells and the foggy blue-and-green sea glass that she collected. On one ledge there were a half dozen combs that she had made from deep-sea scallop shells. She used them to hold her hair back while she swam or when she piled it into a great bun atop her head when she dressed to go to the village.

The seals' very favorite objects of all in the cave were a tin whistle and a *clàrsach*, a small Scottish harp. They loved to hear Ava play. It was not at all like when she spoke a book. It was very different. But this seal and her pup had not come to hear her sing, or to look at the odd curiosities of her land life, or even to eat the smelts that she had so thoughtfully put out for them on the edge of a rock. They had come to tell her a story.

THE CEMETERY

TWO DAYS AFTER HER TERRIBLE NIGHTMARE, May returned to Bar Harbor to pick up some medicine for Zeeba. She had just turned the corner from the doctor's office when she heard someone call from across the street. "May!"

It was Hugh waving and smiling at her. He had a canvas bag slung over his shoulder. There was no avoiding him nor did she want to. But she was still embarrassed about her reaction when he had asked if she wanted to wade. She must have seemed like a complete idiot. She was afraid to look him in the eye as he crossed the street. He put out his hand to shake hers. Would her skin feel odd to him?

"I've spent almost the whole day in the library. I

thought I'd stretch my legs a bit. Would you care to join me on a walk?"

May felt her heart speed up. Was he just trying to be polite? She fiddled with the bag of medicine as she wracked her brain for something to say.

"You seem somewhat preoccupied," he said.

She jerked her head up quickly. "Oh, no . . . I'm not preoccupied at all. Yes, I'll walk with you."

"Is there a place we can sit and talk? It's such a nice day."

"The cemetery," she said quickly.

"The cemetery?" He gave her a curious look.

Had she said the wrong thing? She would try to gather her wits for what sailors called a mid-course correction. "The cemetery is really lovely on a day like this. You feel as if you can see all the way to Ireland."

He tipped his head to one side and looked at her, as if he wasn't sure if he had heard her correctly. Then he smiled. "Why don't you show me?"

As they walked through the stubby stone pillars marking the entrance to the cemetery, their hands brushed against each other. May instantly pulled away and cursed herself. How had she been so careless to let her arms swing about so freely? She should have worn gloves like the fancy summer women and girls who never wanted the sun to touch their white skin. She glanced over at Hugh, scanning his face for any signs of confusion or revulsion. But he hadn't seemed to notice anything strange.

They walked up to the top of the hill. The gravestones, thin and dark, bent into the wind like fragile old folks. The grass whispered softly as if in a private conversation with the bones that lay beneath their roots—a conspiracy between the living and the dead. May stopped briefly in front of a headstone and looked at it. Funny, she had never noticed it before.

"Polly Bunker," Hugh said. "Someone you knew?" Then he chuckled. "How stupid of me. She died in 1873, long before you were born."

"She was a friend of my father's," May said, and then added, "I wish I had known her." A shiver traveled up her spine, and she shrugged her shoulders as if to rid herself of such thoughts.

May and Hugh found a bench and sat down facing the sea. They could see the combers rolling in and breaking on ledges a quarter mile out.

"I see what you mean. It feels like a straight shot to Ireland, doesn't it?"

Hugh draped an arm over the back of the bench. It grazed her shoulders, but she did not flinch. He began to hum a tune.

"What's that you're humming?"

Hugh started to sing in a soft but deep voice as he looked straight out to the horizon, where long purple clouds gathered like schooling whales.

"By yon bonnie banks and by yon bonnie braes,
Where the sun shines bright on Loch Lomond,
Where me and my true love were ever wont to gae,
On the bonnie bonnie banks of Loch Lomond."

May was moved by his voice. The rhythms resonated deep within her, like the lilting cadences of the sea that wrapped around her as she swam.

"That's beautiful. It's an Irish song?" May asked.

"Actually no. It's a Scottish one. I'm not sure if I know any Irish ballads. My family is Scots—but you're close."

May looked at him. Sitting on the bench, humming a ballad, he didn't look like a Harvard man at all. As she watched him stare out at the sea, she began to wonder whether his world was really all that different from hers. *Or,* she thought, *am I just grasping at straws?*

"I like it—Scottish or Irish." She paused. "You have a nice singing voice, too," she said, blushing slightly.

"Did you think an astronomer wouldn't be able to carry a tune?" He smiled. "I also scramble eggs very well." He scratched his chin and looked up at the sky. "And I can do a few card tricks. Let's see what else. I can dance! But I doubt much dancing goes on up here."

"Wrong," May blurted. "There's the apple blossom dance." She hesitated but then said, "You could come if you like."

His gray eyes widened as if he were surprised by

the invitation. "Perhaps, yes. It depends, of course, on how my work is going."

"Yes, of course," May repeated.

Then he turned to her quickly. "Tell me, May, do you know as much about quadrilles as you do about currents?"

May was mortified. It seemed like a jest—perhaps a flirtatious jest—but there could be more to this question. She was immediately defensive. "I am sure you know from all your studies much more about currents than I do from merely reading a single book. So yes, I do know more about quadrilles." She tried to inject a flirtatious note, but it seemed impossible. She was not a very good actress.

Hugh smiled. "Well, when is it?"

"End of the third week in June." There was a thread of hope in her voice.

"But apple blossom time is over by then."

"Not up here on the coast. We're late bloomers."

He laughed hard at this. "Then I'll certainly try to come. It would be a shame not to see you 'late bloomers' in your finery." He reached into his canvas bag and produced the Maury book. "Here," he said, handing it to May. "I thought you might like it back." His hand brushed against hers and she shivered. "I marked an interesting passage in chapter four."

But almost as soon as they had parted ways, May began to worry. Would Hugh really come to the dance? It seemed like almost too much to hope for. By the time she got home with Zeeba's medicine, she was convinced that the last hour had been a dream. She kept trying to picture his smile but it seemed to melt away like ice in sunshine. She tried to recall the timbre of his voice as he sang, but that, too, was as elusive as the last wisps of fog on a brightening morning. And by the time she walked through the door it was as if it had never happened.

"Where the devil have you been? I been waiting here all afternoon for my medicine!"

It never was, it never will be, May thought to herself.

SUMMER 1899

19

THE SHAPE BESIDE ME

MAY HAD A LITTLE MORE THAN A WEEK before the dance. She had almost ceaselessly reviewed all the reasons why Hugh would not come, beginning with *normal girls would never suggest a walk in a cemetery* and ending with her overreaction to his suggestion of wading. Why had she not simply said that she was just getting over a cold and didn't want to wade? That, of course, would be hindsight. But foresight wasn't much better. She imagined him coming to the dance and falling for a lively, flirtatious girl like Lottie Beal. Lottie was irresistible. Dimpled, blond curls, and by no means dumb! But she did not spend hours on end in the library reading science books, either. And she was human—wholly, totally human.

It was hard for May to believe that for the brief time she and Hugh had sat together on the cemetery bench, she had felt so at peace. But she had swum more and farther in these last two weeks since he had gone. Had the sea laid a deeper claim on her? One that could not be missed? Should she resist the sea between now and the dance? Might Hugh, like Rudd, look at her suspiciously? She thought of that horrible moment when Rudd had watched her as she picked up the math papers and said in that flat voice, *"Guess she'll have to go swimming for the rest."* She could never imagine Hugh speaking as Rudd had, but would Hugh sense something odd about her and begin to withdraw?

She could tolerate Rudd's suspicions, but not Hugh's. Would he think she was a freak if he knew of her secret life? Had her skin felt abnormal when their hands had brushed against each other? She knew she had recoiled at that moment, but had he?

The questions haunted her, and soon she found herself caught in a maze of conflicting emotions that were laced through with a mortifying guilt.

Maybe, she thought, she really should try not going into the sea between now and the dance. It would be hard, but at least she should try.

So for two nights she resisted going to "the visible ocean." And every single hour of every single day and night she was caught in an endless cycle of yearning and self-recrimination, of denial and longing. On the third night of not swimming, she noticed that she had begun to itch fiercely. But every time she considered giving in, she imagined herself at the dance—dancing with Hugh. She saw no other dancers on the floor—just herself and Hugh, swirling about. She would wear her hair down with a green ribbon that matched her eyes woven through it.

Before she knew it she had a fever.

When she walked into the kitchen her father looked up at her in alarm.

"May, de-ah. Good gracious, you look like you're burning up."

"I don't feel very well, Pa." She began to sway. He ran to her and caught her just before she sank to the floor.

"You're hot as a brick in a kiln and look at your skin—it's got some awful red rash."

At that moment Zeeba appeared. "What's happening here? What's wrong with May?"

"She's sick, Zeeba. She's got a high fever. And look—her hands are all red."

"Well, get her away from me. I can't afford to catch anything. That's just how my grandmother died. She was down with her weak heart and some influenza broke loose in town and, well, her heart couldn't fight the fever. Hopeless. Completely hopeless."

"I'm taking her right into the doctor is what I'm doing."

Although the weather was warm May was shivering so hard her teeth were chattering. Her father wrapped her in two blankets and half carried, half dragged her down to the skiff. By the time they reached Bar Harbor, May was delirious. The one thing she was vaguely aware of were those twin spaces on either side of her. The two voids were pressing hotly against her.

When she regained consciousness, she was in

Dr. Holmes's office. The doctor, her father, and Dr. Holmes's wife were peering over her.

"May! May? Can you hear us?"

"Yes, yes . . . What happened to me?"

"Well, May." A wan smile crossed the doctor's face like a fleeting shadow. "Thank heavens your fever has broken."

"How long have I been here?"

"Three hours, just about," Mrs. Holmes said.

"You seem much better," Dr. Holmes said. "Your fever is down, but your rash still looks fairly severe. I think you need to bathe with mineral oil. I'll give you a good supply. You need to put a cupful in with your bathwater. Then put on a lotion that I'll give you at least three times a day. I'm not sure what caused this. It's not contagious."

"Zeeba will be relieved about that," Gar muttered.

"Well, May can certainly stay here tonight with my wife and me. We could keep an eye on her."

May knew exactly what caused this illness and the last thing she needed was mineral oils or lotions or Dr. Holmes and his wife keeping an eye on her.

She had to get back to the sea as quickly as possible. Her experiment had failed, had almost killed her. *How stupid!* May thought. *Stupid of me. I went against my own nature. That's what is sick!*

"That's kind of you, Doctor Holmes, but I think I'd feel better if I were at home in my own bed."

"That's perfectly understandable, dear," Mrs. Holmes said. "But you just follow Doctor Holmes's advice with the baths and the lotion."

⚜ ⚜ ⚜

"You brought her back?" Zeeba shrieked as Gar and May walked through the door.

"She's better, and she's not contagious."

"Just like that she's better!" Zeeba snapped her fingers in the air. "Well, I'll be! That girl's strong as a horse. I told you. One minute burning up with a fever, next fit as a fiddle. May, better start supper. I'll cut the potatoes. You fry up the bacon."

"Stop right there, Zeeba," Gar said, in a low, firm voice.

"What are you telling me to stop for?"

"She ain't going to be cooking no supper. She's

going to take a bath with this here oil that doctor gave her and then she's going to put on some lotion he gave her."

"He gave her medicine? Prescription medicine?" There was a trace of disbelief in her voice, as if Zeeba could not understand that someone aside from herself was worthy of a prescription.

"He did indeed."

"Must have cost." She turned and walked toward the stove, grumbling.

May took the bath as Dr. Holmes had told her to. And, as she knew, it had no effect on the rash whatsoever. She just had to wait until her parents had gone to sleep, then she would slip out of the house and down to the water. It was a perfect night for swimming. Moonless, hardly a breeze. No one would see her.

Finally May heard her father climb the steps of the tower to wind the clockworks for the last time and check the kerosene. She would give him twenty minutes after he came down and then go.

As soon as she dove into the surf she felt the last of the fever leave her body. The terrible itching stopped. She was back, back in her own skin! And as she swam straight out to sea those two voids on either side of her that had pressed like hot irons began to assume a somewhat familiar shape. She was not sure why she felt they were familiar, but she sensed a companionable intimacy about them, and they seemed to acquire a new vitality and immediacy.

The farther she swam, the more May was aware that something was coming closer. Not to swim, to resist the sea, was unthinkable—indeed, shameful. Once May had marveled that there were so many shades of gray, but now she was perplexed by the myriad shades of shame. She was caught between her own mortification of her not-quite-human life and the even deeper shame in denying it.

She felt that she had literally swum back into her own skin; she could not swim far enough. She was amazed by her own speed. There was an eagle flying overhead when she finally turned to swim back to Egg Rock. Gar had told her once that eagles were among the fastest long-distance fliers of any birds. May was pressed to get home quickly as the day was about to break. She passed the eagle easily and was ahead of him by several lengths the rest of the way back to Egg Rock.

The next morning, fully recovered, May went down to the beach and stood on the very edge of the sloping rock, peering straight out to sea—southeast, the route she had taken the night before. She had not realized how powerfully she could swim until that night. And to think she had started off sick and fever-ish! She felt a certain sense of pride. Had she let that tide take her, it would have swept her to the south-ern tip of Nova Scotia—Cape Sable Island. This was the outer limit of the Bay of Maine. Beyond it was the open ocean. She wondered how far and how long she could have swum. Could she have gone across the Atlantic?

She closed her eyes tight for a moment and imagined the large chart that hung in the lighthouse. Cape Sable resembled the large clawed foot of a bird, three talons hanging off into the Bay of Maine. If one swam a bit north and due east one would reach Ireland, then a bit farther north one would come to Scotland. There was a sprinkling of islands off the western coast of Scotland. It seemed like a cozier place than Ireland, with all those islands and the countless inlets and coves. It seemed like Maine, actually. Islands were more inviting. And, of course, on an island one was never far from the sea whereas on a continent . . . She did not finish the thought but opened her eyes as she heard the chuffing of a steamer coming through the Egg Rock passage.

It was the *Elizabeth M. Prouty* from Boston. A sure sign of summer. The rich people sent up their house staffs early to get their "cottages" ready. Their cottages were ten times larger than any house lived in by the year-round folk of Bar Harbor. But for some reason there was a time-honored insistence by these people to call them "cottages." Despite elaborate gardens, gleaming yachts, upstairs maids, downstairs maids, and butlers, they considered coming to Mount Desert Island, Maine, an experiment in "rustic living."

Suddenly May felt a deep thrilling vibration course through her body. One space beside her seemed to fill with a radiant cool mist. A throbbing light only she could see emanated from the deck of the *Elizabeth M. Prouty* to engulf her. She opened her eyes wide and stared ahead. There was a flash of sunlit amber that sparkled in the dawn light.

"It's her!" May said. No one else was on deck except a willowy girl who appeared to float weightlessly as she leaned over the railing. Long tendrils of her hair had blown loose in the breeze and streamed across her face, slightly obscuring her features. Was this the face she had seen through the porthole of the *Josiah B. Harwood*? Had her kin come to Bar Harbor? May was so frightened, however, that this time she did not raise her hand as she had in front of the porthole. The reflection had waved back, but if this girl did would it mean that she was a mere illusion, another watery specter? And what if she didn't wave back? What would that mean? May felt a tightening in her stomach and a ghost of a flutter in her feet just where her flukes formed when she was in the sea.

Would it mean that she was the only one? That she would swim forever alone in this vast ocean?

Maybe this girl on the *Elizabeth M. Prouty* was just a haughty rich visitor who called her mansion a "cottage." May tried her best to prepare herself for disappointment. Then a truly dreadful thought came to her. *Maybe she is rich and beautiful, more beautiful than I am and completely human.* And Hugh would meet her at one of the fancy parties and fall in love with her and there would be no division between them because she was a land person and not mer.

May walked back up to the lighthouse. When she entered she found Zeeba in the kitchen. She was up earlier than usual, clattering about. Indeed she was almost bustling, or as close to bustling as Hepzibah ever could get.

"Well, I can see you're all better!" This veered closer to being an accusation than a mere comment. "Oh, and by the way. You shouldn't leave your schoolbooks out."

"What? What are you talking about?" May asked.

"That oil done got knocked over and spilled on them."

"What oil?"

"The oil the doctor gave you. It got knocked over." She jerked her head toward the table where May often did her homework.

"Zeeba!" May shrieked. "This isn't a schoolbook. It's a library book!"

"Library, school—what's the difference?" She looked up at May, a wild glimmer in her eyes. May was aghast. It was Maury's *The Physical Geography of the Sea.* She had planned to give it back to Hugh at the dance. What would he think of her now? The book's lovely green cover had an ugly dark oily stain spread across it. She had remembered Hugh's hand when he had given her the book with the bookmark. And now the bookmark was gone! A bookmark didn't just move on its own.

May picked up the book and pressed it to her chest as if it were an injured infant. Then she turned and walked right up to Zeeba. "You're crazy!"

"Don't you go calling me crazy, girl!" she hissed.

"'That oil done got knocked over!'" May mocked her words. "You knocked it over. That book was not on the table. It was on the shelf by my bed. The oil was by the bath. When you decide to pull a nasty trick like that, cover your tracks better."

Zeeba's eyes began to roll back in her head. It was as if she were a snake coiling up ready to strike. But May wasn't afraid. She knew she had won this round, and as if to confirm it, Gar had witnessed what had just transpired.

"Zeeba, go to bed. Just take your damn tonics, your tablets, your powders, and go to bed."

It was as if the woman folded in on herself and shrank before their very eyes. She scuttled out of the room, clutching her jar of powders.

"WHO NAMES THE STARS?"

"**THERE YOU ARE!**" Hugh Fitzsimmons greeted her as she entered the Odd Fellows Hall. May was wearing the same jacket and blue skirt as she had to the earlier dance, but she had her hair fixed differently. It was fetched up on top of her head with a comb that she had fashioned from a scallop shell she had found far out and very deep. It was flatter than most scallop shells, and the ribbed edges of its fan were deeply indented. She had used a file of her father's to cut them a bit deeper, which made it a perfect comb. Although she had looked forward more than anything to seeing Hugh at this dance, her emotions were in a tangle.

Her "experiment," as she now thought of her attempt to resist going to sea, had failed, and none of her fears had subsided in the least. The summer folks were beginning to stream in, and although she had not seen the girl from the *Elizabeth M. Prouty* in town, she had seen other pretty summer visitors and all of them fully human!

And on top of everything there was the oil-stained Maury book. How would she explain that? The damage wasn't as bad as she had thought. Gar had shown her a very clever trick that had lessened the stain somewhat. He took several spoonfuls of flour and pressed it onto the cover. The flour absorbed the oil and this had diminished the stain appreciably, but there were traces of it still there, just as there might be traces of her secret life swirling about her being. Her own "stain," the rash, had subsided completely, but were there other telltale signs that might betray her? Then she had another thought that was truly alarming. What if he was only drawn to her because of this oddity? He was a scientist, after all.

What if she became an object of scientific investigation? A specimen! The last thing May wanted to be was Hugh Fitzsimmons's experiment. She barely had time to organize her thoughts after his greeting when she felt a sharp tap on her shoulder. "You weren't late this time and already dancing with some-one, eh?"

It was Rudd. Her heart sank. How could this be happening? Well, at least she had a response. "I'm not dancing with anyone. I just got here, as you said."

"Well, talking with someone." He slid his eyes toward Hugh.

"Talking isn't dancing," May protested softly. But Hugh stepped forward and thrust out his hand in a friendly manner.

"Hello. Hugh Fitzsimmons."

"From away, I take it," Rudd said.

How rude!

"Mr. Fitzsimmons is from Cambridge, Massa-chusetts. He is an astronomer and has come here to make some astronomical observations."

"Come all this way for the stars?" Rudd asked, and snorted.

"You can observe them from Boston and Cambridge. But you know what they call this region of Maine—the place where the earth meets the sky—for it is where the daylight first strikes our country. Mount Abenaki, just over there." Hugh cocked his head in the direction of one of Maine's tallest peaks.

"I know where it is," Rudd said bluntly. The message was clear. *I don't need someone from away to tell me what's in my own backyard.*

"Of course there is a lot of fog, but when it's clear, there is no place like it. Miss Plum and I met in the library."

"Oh, she likes all that book learnin'. She particularly likes meeting men in the library who can—"

"Rudd! What are you saying?" May broke in.

"Didn't you tell me that Doctor Holmes done taught you some higher mathematics there?"

"Yes, he was there. He came in after me that day and tried to explain some equations." What did she have to explain to Rudd or to Hugh for that matter? She felt a fury rising in her. Her green eyes were bright as emeralds. And one might have seen tears. However, they did not look like liquid, but flecks of diamonds.

Rudd seemed slightly unnerved. He thrust his

hand into his pocket and drew out a quarter. "What do you say we flip for the first dance; fair enough?"

May felt her hand curl into a fist. But there was something she noticed in Rudd's eyes that disturbed her. It was as if there were a dead spot, a vacant space behind those dark eyes — a hollowness into which all feeling or connection to feelings would wither.

Then Hugh spoke in a voice she would have never guessed him to possess. It was so different, with none of the buoyancy, the good-humored casualness that seemed to characterize his speech. "I don't believe young women are objects for betting."

"Huh." It was a dismissive, rude sound. "I guess you can say I'm just a gambling man." May looked at Rudd's face. It seemed wrong, strange, as if the person behind it had just left and simply didn't live there anymore.

"You gamble with things, sir, not human beings," Hugh replied.

May felt something seize up in her. She turned and rushed from the hall. The tears that had threatened for the last three minutes spilled, liquid and salty. They stung like no seawater she had swum in as they coursed down her face.

She was out the door before either one could stop her but she was not sure where to go. Miss Lowe, she knew, had gone to her sister's in Brunswick. Everyone else was at the dance. She was stuck. She could swim home, but that was hardly a solution. She had told her father that someone would sail her back— she was careful not to specify whom, for indeed she had been hoping that Hugh would be there and knew for certain Rudd would. And now she didn't want either of them to take her. Those last words of Hugh's rang in her ears. *"You gamble with things, not human beings." But if I am not human, am I a thing . . . just a thing?*

She felt a hot shame wash through her.

"May! May!" She had been crying so hard she had not heard the footsteps behind her. "May, wait up!" It was Hugh. She couldn't let him see her like this. "May, honestly!" he cried, and it was perhaps the note of exasperation in his voice that slowed her. She looked around. His hair was disheveled and he was panting.

"Good lord, you're in better condition than I am." His face cracked into that wonderful smile. She felt something melt inside her. He put both his hands gently on her shoulders. Then his face turned serious. "That was very ugly back there, but none of this is your fault."

She looked down, afraid to meet his gaze. As he began to speak she caught the glimmer of something. Caught in the weave of her very plain shawl were perhaps half a dozen flattened little crystals that sparkled in the thick darkness of the night. *My teardrops!* They had stung fiercely when she had shed them, but they were no longer liquid. They were like the flattened ovals she had collected from the sea chest. And there were a few on the ground as well. She wiped her face. Panic welled up in her. He could not see this! He simply could not. How would she explain it? "May, let me take you home. It's a beautiful night for a sail. The boat sails so well."

She sniffed and wiped her eyes with her hand, not her shawl. "Yes, some say Phineas is a better boatbuilder than his father." They began to walk toward the wharf.

"Phineas loves wood. You can tell it. I spent several hours over there before I left, watching him plane pieces for that big yacht they are building."

"Yes, it's for the *Merrillee*—for some rich people from New York." Her voice was taut, but she was trying hard to appear normal. She still had not looked up. They had fallen into step beside each other. Once again she had the sensation as she walked that she was slightly outside of her own body, moving along beside herself. But Hugh did not pick up on her anxiety. He was talking in an easy way. The ugliness from the hall began to recede.

"Phineas has even made me this wonderful contraption so I can set my telescope in it and keep it steady. I was hoping to try it out tonight. It is very calm; the sea is fairly flat."

"There's a cove on the back side of Egg Rock that never gets stirred up. It's protected, you know."

"Would you show it to me, May?"

May hesitated a moment and stared at her shoes. Then she raised her face and looked into the loveliness of his gray eyes. "If you like."

"I would like that very much." He took her hand in his.

✿   ✿   ✿

A half hour later they glided into the protected cove and dropped anchor. "Let me just set things up. You'll see how clever this is. That Phineas is really something."

For the next several minutes Hugh was absorbed in securing the mount and brackets for the telescope. This gave May the opportunity to check carefully to see if any of the crystallized teardrops were in evidence. She found one or two and quickly flicked them into the water. She noticed that they glimmered and cast minuscule little halos around them. Then they seemed to dissolve completely.

"All right," Hugh said as he pressed his eyes to the scope. "Let's see what's up there tonight." May leaned her head back against the gunwales of the boat and looked straight up. The sash of the Milky Way unspooled like a broad pale ribbon through the night. Nonetheless she was aware of Hugh. He moved lightly in the boat. When she shifted her gaze away from the sky she noticed that his gestures were smooth and economical. There was an ineffable grace to his every move and the boat hardly rocked as he adjusted the telescope. It was odd because although Rudd was bigger, bulkier, she was infinitely more aware of Hugh's physical presence. It did not intrude, but she felt wrapped in his grace in the same way she felt wrapped in the water when she first dove in.

"I see Aldebaran, so the Pleiades must be already up, but I can't quite see them yet. Of course, August is the best time to view them this far north."

"Why? I saw them the other night."

"You did?"

"Just rising." She suddenly realized she had said too much. "You know, from the watch room of the lighthouse."

"Even with the flashes from the light you could see them?"

She had to think fast. "Well, I thought I saw them; perhaps I was mistaken."

"One easy way to find them is to first search out Aldebaran because it follows the Pleiades." He paused while he adjusted the lens. "Yes, I've got Aldebaran, but there is a bit of cloud cover higher up, so I think we'll not get a good view, but come take a look. I'll show you Aldebaran. Have you ever seen it before?"

"I probably have but didn't know it." May smiled.

"All right, I know you have looked through a telescope, being a light keeper's daughter. So you just twist that ring until it focuses properly for you. Now you can see Taurus—the bull that looks nothing like a bull to my mind."

"What does it look like?"

"A stick figure leaning back on its knees and waving its arms around."

May laughed softly. "You're right! Who names the stars?"

"Everyone, or at least every culture seems to take a crack at it. Aldebaran means *follower* in Arabic, which is logical, seeing as it does follow the Pleiades, but some have called it *the Driver* and I can't remember, but the Babylonians, I think, called it *Fat Camel*."

"Why?"

"I don't know. You'd have to ask them."

"Fat chance."

Hugh laughed at this. She wished she could have turned to see his face, but her eye was pressed against the eyepiece of the telescope. Then from the corner of her eye, or was it the lens, she caught a flitting silver shadow of something familiar—not a stick figure. It looked like the tail—her tail when she swam, glittering and sweeping through the night sky.

"I just saw something for a split second but it's gone now."

"A shooting star?" Hugh asked.

"No. I mean it's not gone. I think I just nudged the telescope accidentally and now I can't see it."

"Let's have a look."

May stepped away and felt his hand steady her. They changed places. She readjusted the scallop comb in her hair. "That's so pretty. What is it?" Hugh asked as she dug the comb just beneath the thick knot of hair.

"Scallop shell, I think." Once again she felt she had said too much and tried to shift the conversation back to astronomy. "What's that constellation to the right of Aldebaran?"

"Did you know," Hugh said, and softly touched the scallop comb, "that the scallop shell was worn by pilgrims in Europe when they made their journeys to the shrine of Saint James in Spain?"

What doesn't Hugh know? May thought. His knowledge seemed infinite. While she was thinking this she felt him edge closer to her. She could feel his warm breath brush her cheek. She was no longer looking at Aldebaran but down at the floorboards of the boat, afraid to look up at the sky or even to slide her gaze to the side. Her heart raced. It seemed to her that it was an all too human heart that was beating in her chest.

The palms of his hands gently stroked her cheeks, then cradled her head as he kissed her lips. The stars spun in the night. The world seemed to change in that instant. Nothing was where it should be or had been. The horizon might have swept up to the moon, and the moon might have changed color. With the first touch of their lips, the boundaries between their worlds dissolved. For May it was as if the stars rearranged themselves and the constellations scrambled into new geometries that defied their names.

"The gifts of the night" was what Hugh called the stars, and they were nothing compared to the wealth of feelings that was growing between May and Hugh for each other.

Hugh not only knew about the science of the stars but he knew poetry. And that first night he recited a verse from memory by a poet she had never heard of named William Blake. The poem was about a "fair-hair'd angel of the evening." Hugh promised to bring her a book of Blake's poetry the next time they met, "since you are my 'fair-hair'd angel.'"

"But I'm not fair-haired," she said, taking a long, thick strand that had fallen from the scallop comb. "I'm not sure if red counts."

"Of course it does," he replied, and picked up the strand and pressed it to his lips. "I suppose you're going to tell me you're not an angel, either."

A shiver passed up her spine, and she gave a small shake. She wrapped her arms around her shoulders.

"Cold?"

"No, no," she said in barely a whisper. *Not cold, but not quite an angel*, she thought.

When Hugh returned to the small dinghy dock in the village and neatened up the boat, he sat for several minutes, thinking. There was something so extraordinary about May. She had a quick mind, one of the quickest he had ever encountered. She was every bit as smart as any of the Radcliffe College girls he had met, and yet she'd received much less formal education. By her own admission there were long periods of time when she missed school because it was impossible to get to Bar Harbor from the lighthouse. And yet she had read the entire volume of Maury's *Physical Geography of the Sea*. And she mentioned that she had been trying to teach herself trigonometry. When she'd given him the book, she'd apologized if there were any scraps of paper still stuck between the pages.

But it was not simply her intellect that impressed him. There was something essentially mysterious about her. She was like the stars—alluring and yet ultimately unknowable. Even her hair was unique, a shade he had never seen. It was the color of cooling embers, full of subtle flickers, soft radiances. However it was her eyes, with their green intensity, that held the secret of her being, the mystery that was at her center. He had kissed her. He hadn't meant to. But he did and it was . . . His thoughts drifted off. She was beyond words. He sighed and looked down. Something glittered on the floorboards of the boat. He reached down and picked it up. Was it a fish scale? How would a fish scale have gotten into the boat? He was the first person to sail it, the only so far. Well, he knew they scaled fish on the next pier over. So perhaps the wind just blew the scales around a bit. He was just about to flick it overboard, but something stopped him and instead he tucked it into his pocket.

SHADES OF GRAY

"YOU SEEM MIGHTY PERKY," Zeeba said when May walked into the kitchen the morning following the dance.

"Oh, I guess it's just summer coming on. Makes me feel good."

Zeeba made one of her half sigh, half groan noises. It was a sound May often thought must be difficult to make for it seemed to come simultaneously from both Hepzibah's chest and her nose. May made a habit of never responding to this odd noise. "I think I'll go out and check the new chicks."

They had ordered chicken eggs, which had been delivered four weeks before, and they had only just hatched. "They don't need your tending them yet.

They're just a day old. Don't need to feed a chick 'til it's three days old." Zeeba was right. May knew this. Just before a chicken hatches it draws into its stomach all the yolk of the egg from which it hatched. They arrive well fed. But May wanted to get out of the house. She wanted to relive those kisses of the night before.

Here it was summer—clear blue sky—and yet inside the lighthouse it seemed like the dead of winter. Zeeba had closed most of the curtains, for she said that the light hurt her failing eyes. Murky shadows crowded every corner of the house. Dimness lurked in every nook and cranny.

There were so many shades of gray. There was the bleak, leaden grayness of the lighthouse—repressive, gloomy, deadening. Then there was the clear gray of Hugh Fitzsimmons's eyes. Lively, full of light, like a breaking dawn.

May went out to the chicken yard. The chicks seemed fine—twenty little hatchlings all softly bobbing about. She sat down and picked up one. Holding it in her hands, she could feel its rapidly beating heart. It seemed to soothe her jumbled emotions about Hugh. She had never felt this way about any boy . . . *well, he's not really a boy*, she thought. *He's a young man and so is Rudd.* She might have liked Rudd well enough once. But now she could hardly believe she ever had. Why hadn't she seen through Rudd's confidence to realize it was really cockiness? Hugh was confident, too, sure of himself but never cocky. He could laugh at himself. She bet that Rudd could never do that. The question came back to haunt her once again — *What if Hugh knew that I am not quite human? Would he be sickened?* Suddenly it was as if the light drained out of the day. She could never tell Hugh Fitzsimmons who she really was. Never, ever.

And what if he doesn't really like me at all? What if I am just a passing fancy, something to entertain him while he does his research in Maine? Then what matter would it make what I am? There must be so many beautiful, fashionable girls in Boston, smarter than she was, more elegant.

That night, as she slipped into the water, she felt guilty. Was she swimming to her life or away from it? The sea was so still that the reflections of the stars barely shivered. But for the first time since her transformation, she felt a kind of loss. She was leaving behind the world that Hugh Fitzsimmons knew and entering one that he could never, despite all his learning, even imagine. She swam on slowly.

The two dolphins that now often swam with her were not swimming as close as usual. They seemed to sense that she was in no mood for play tonight. She needed to be alone, so they soon grew bored and swam off.

When she was well past The Bones, May rolled over on her back. She lifted her tail and studied it in a shaft of moonlight. Was it freakish? The scales climbed up over her hips and finished in a curve just beneath her navel. Would a human find her revolting? Would her shape, her form, disgust Hugh? She had never felt lonelier.

Yet she was not entirely alone. Once again she felt the two empty spaces on each side of her pressing in. She looked up at the stars and searched for the

Seven Sisters of the Pleiades. The moon was still young, so the darkness made the star cluster more visible. She found two of the sisters just rising on the purple line of the horizon.

"Have you ever loved?" She spoke out loud to them as if she expected the stars to whisper back to her. "Loved a human?" She swam through the night and into the clear gray light of the dawn.

A STRANGE ENCOUNTER

A WEEK LATER, May was walking down the street in the village when she spied Rudd ahead. Abruptly she turned into a small lane to avoid him. She couldn't forget his face from the night of the dance. The vacant space behind the eyes that made him— the words popped into her head—*less than human.* But was that not exactly what she was? A chill ran through her.

"Hannah!" She felt a tap on her shoulder. Surely it couldn't be him. He had been at least a hundred yards away. She wheeled around, a seething fury rising in her. It was not Rudd but a tall, dark-haired man with luminous green eyes. But those eyes soon clouded in confusion. "P-pardon me," he stammered.

"I mistook you for someone else." The color drained from his face. He seemed suddenly fearful and wavered slightly on his feet. He was holding a small jug of something that he had apparently just bought at the chandlery.

"Are you all right?" May said. The man looked as if he were suffering some sort of attack.

"No! No! I'm fine. Really." The color crept back into his face and he laughed, although it seemed rather forced. "It's just that you do resemble another young lady—and—and I'm slightly embarrassed."

"Oh" was all May could think to say. She was uncomfortable with the way he was regarding her. It was not offensive by any means, and yet it seemed slightly intrusive, as if he saw something in her? Once again, she was aware of a cool radiance that seemed to define those spaces at her sides. She looked at the man again. He didn't seem like a shipyard worker; perhaps he was a yacht captain and that was why he had been in the chandlery shop. She looked at the jug.

"Turpentine," he said. "Painter, you know." His eyes were clamped on her face as if he were searching for something, or perhaps attempting to convince himself that she was not the other girl. She suddenly realized that there was an odd familiarity about him. She had never seen him before, of this she was certain, but there was something about this man that resonated within her.

"Painter? Yacht painter?"

"Oh, no, portrait painter. I am doing a portrait of the Hawleys' daughters."

"Oh, summer folk," she said, thinking of all the beautifully dressed girls who would soon be fawning over Hugh.

"Yes."

There was nothing left to say. There never was much to say between island people and the summer folk, except if they served in their "cottages." And a portrait painter did not qualify as a servant. May realized this. She knew of the Hawleys. They had a vast, rambling estate that was called Gladrock. She said good-bye and walked quickly down the lane. But she felt the painter's eyes on her back the entire time.

Impossible! Stannish Whitman Wheeler thought as he watched May turn the corner at the end of the lane. *How on earth could there be two of them?* As soon as she turned around, he knew it was not Hannah, although the resemblance was extraordinary. But he was a portrait painter. He knew faces. In the manner that cartographers could map an unknown continent and transpose a landscape, a topography, from the mysterious into the knowable, he could interpret the geography of a face and map it with his paints and brushes. The girl's chin was a tad less sharp, but had the same slight dimple in the middle. Her cheekbones a degree or two higher. Her eyebrows did not sweep in with quite the same curvature. And the mouth? Perhaps a bit less generous. Yet she moved with the same fluid grace as Hannah.

And there was one thing he knew for certain. This girl, unlike Hannah, had already crossed over. She knew what she was. As if to confirm this she wore a scallop shell—the scallop of the Cailleach, found in the deep open waters of the Atlantic, which rarely washed up on any beach. The word *Cailleach* meant *blue hag* or *veiled one* in Scottish folklore. And the pleated shell, which was almost pure white with reddish or blue tints at its edges, did resemble a veil or mantle like a nun's wimple or a priestly stole.

God forbid, he thought, *that a man falls in love with her as I have with Hannah.* "God forbid!" And this time he whispered it aloud.

He felt someone touch his shoulder and wheeled around. He was embarrassed to be caught talking to himself. He hoped this rugged fellow hadn't heard him.

"Pardon me, mister, but did you see a gal with red hair pass this way?"

"Girl with red hair?" he repeated. Something about the man's face unnerved him. "I'm not sure."

"Either she did or she didn't, mister. It ain't such a hard question."

Stannish Wheeler was indeed a knower of faces. His eyes scrutinized the one before him. There was something about the man that was disturbing.

Predatory. "No," he said quickly. "I was talking to a woman, not a young girl, just a minute ago, but she had jet-black hair. Not red. About thirty, thirty-five years old, I would say."

"Not the one I'm hunting," Rudd said quickly, and went off.

Hunting! Stannish Wheeler thought. And although the man went in the opposite direction, the painter felt only small relief.

OPPOSITE SHORES

MAY'S FATHER HAD BEGUN TO ALLOW HER to take the skiff to and from Egg Rock on her own when the weather was good. She was not sure why he had come to this decision. It might have been for the same reasons that he was so agreeable to her meeting Hugh at the cove beach. After a few of these evening meetings she decided to tell her father about their star sails, as she called them. Gar seemed genuinely happy for her. But they both agreed that it was perhaps not a good idea to tell Zeeba.

Her sense was that Gar had agreed partly in defiance of Zeeba. For ever since that day when Hepzibah had said so quietly and yet with such deadly earnestness, "You're not mine," a new power was unleashed in May. As horrible as those words might have seemed, they gave her the power to call her life her own.

May would never openly defy Gar, but it was as if her father almost envied her for claiming ownership of her life in a way he never had. He was both amazed and inspired by her boldness, and he wanted to honor it. There came to be a tacit understanding between May and Gar that Hepzibah's position in the household had changed. Her complications, her elaborately contrived physical failures, were failures of not eyes, heart, or lungs but failures of the soul.

Hepzibah Plum sensed this change in her position as much as anyone. Although May and Gar still brought her hot-water bottles, fetched all the potions, powders, and tonics, spared her any of the normal household chores that a woman might be expected to perform, Hepzibah felt that her complications were no longer respected. May and Gar indulged her as one might indulge a very young child who claimed to have an imaginary friend. They played along, and it enraged Hepzibah.

Hepzibah was home alone at the moment. Gar had gone out with Doug Hardy to help him haul traps, and the girl had gone off in the skiff. Hepzibah was deeply suspicious of May whenever she left and was sure she was sneaking off to see a boy. Well, if she got herself in the family way they'd have to hire someone to help out. The idea of May going off and marrying used to upset Hepzibah. But ever since the change in the household, this lack of respect for her complications, she had begun to think perhaps it would be better to get a hired girl in. Her cousin Suzanne, out in western Massachusetts, had a daughter, a docile dough-faced girl, Iris, who might fit the bill fine. They wouldn't have to pay her much, not if they provided room and board.

Hepzibah got up from her rocker to shut the screen door, which was flapping about in the breeze. Gar should have fixed the durn thing weeks ago. She didn't like drafts slipping in uninvited. And those chicks were peeping out there. She bet the girl had forgotten to feed them. Well, Hepzibah would do it. Serve the girl right if one of those pullet chicks died. Then where would they be next winter for eggs?

After tending to the pullets, Hepzibah walked around to the other side of the house to see if she could spot either Gar or May coming back. It was long past dinnertime.

She raised her hand to her forehead to shade her eyes and scanned the cut between the island and Bar Harbor. She spotted the gaff-rigged sail of the skiff and pressed her lips together. "Hmmph." It would take May another forty-five minutes to get back on this wind. She would have to tack against it. So much for dinner!

Hepzibah plopped down on the round top of a large spool that had been used for cable and decided to watch her. "Girl's got a way with the wind," she muttered as she saw May neatly come into the wind and head off on a new tack. As the skiff drew closer she could make out May's figure at the tiller. *What is that fool thing she wears in her hair all the time?*

There were other boats out there that were wrestling with the shifting and capricious breezes, but May seemed to be slipping right through them. It was as if she were playing cat's cradle with the wind. She avoided becoming tangled while the others were floundering about, luffing to a near halt as their sails were pressed into irons and not pulling worth a tinker's damn. "Way with the wind," Hepzibah murmured again, and then began to wonder some more.

Hepzibah tipped her head toward the sunshine and closed her eyes. Did she think of Polly Bunker first or Noggy Brynn? Or did they both come to her at the same time? But Polly was real, very real. Didn't matter that she had been dead all these years. She'd been Gar's true love, his fiancée, and she'd clung to him from the grave, she had! Sometimes Hepzibah swore she could smell Polly—a sick, rotting-flesh stench. She knew Gar visited her grave up at the Meeting House cemetery, where all the Bunkers done been planted. Not her family, thank God. She didn't want to be neighborly with Polly in death. It was bad enough now with Polly dead and her alive!

And Noggy? Well, that was just an old tale about a sea witch who lived in a cave off Grand Manan. But they were both beautiful. Noggy, the stories went, had strange powers over the tide, the moon, and yes, the wind—a way with the wind. She had a magic rope tied with three knots—witches' knots they called them—the first could summon a gentle breeze, the second a southeasterly, and the third a strong nor'easter full of ice and fury even in the summer. Polly Bunker had her ways, too, not perhaps with the wind but with men. Was it possible for Polly to have birthed the girl? She died in the winter. She could have hidden her pregnancy, but no. Not possible, for it was ten years later that Gar had brought the baby back, and it was a baby—not a ten-year-old child. She laughed.

"Whatcha laughing about out here in the sun, Zeeba?" May had been astonished to come across Zeeba sitting on the spool, looking perhaps more relaxed, almost content, than she had ever seen her. Hepzibah leaped up. Her energy and quickness stunned May. "What's come over you, Zeeba?"

For a few seconds Hepzibah appeared slightly disoriented. Then her eyes hardened and she glared at May. "Whatcha got there in your hand?"

"Well, in this hand I got your new stomach powders from Doctor Holmes."

"I mean the other hand!" Hepzibah spoke sharply. "And no lying."

"No lying? What are you talking about? It's a halyard from the skiff. It's starting to shred. I took it down so Pa can splice it."

"It's got three knots in it," Hepzibah said in an accusatory voice.

"Yes, so what? I tried to fix it just temporary."

"Just temporary?" She made the low growlish sound she so often summoned to express disapproval mixed with disbelief. "You want to know what I got?" Hepzibah plunged her hand into a deep pocket in the folds of her skirt. "Now, lookee here!" She opened her hand to reveal a dead chick. "You done starved it, girl. You ain't been doing your chores."

May felt a nausea seize hold of her. Her legs turned weak. Something was very wrong with Hepzibah.

Somewhere above them a seagull screeched and wheeled through the sky.

May had done her chores. That chick had not starved to death. Its neck was broken.

Ever since the seal and her pup had come to Avalonia's cave and told her the garbled story about the mer creature who had saved the seal pup's life, Avalonia had been tormented. Although she had tried to understand it as best she could, the story came out in such a disjointed, confused muddle there was no way she could unscramble any of the details. She could not figure out where they had come from. Was it from the north, the Shetlands, through the Caledonia passage to the North Sea, or the south or the west? But surely a mother and pup would not have come all that way from the west, across the Atlantic. Unless, of course, they had caught the current that mer folk knew about that was embedded deep in the Gulf Stream. But that was only for mer folk. No other creatures traveled it. Would the mer creature who helped them have told them about the Avalaur current? It was the current for which she and her sister had been named, and it began in and looped back to the gyre of Corry.

The story the seal told her became splinters of glass digging at the old fears and memories she had so neatly tucked away. For days on end Avalonia could not sleep. Her dreams were fractured with shards of old nightmares. It had been so long since Laurentia had died—died in her own arms on that deserted beach. But Avalonia had promised to search for the babes. And she had for days until it became too dangerous. First she had been sighted by a boat from the Marine Revenue Service and then been chased by a trawler. The trawl nets hung from the booms, ready to drop and sweep her up. She had only the fog to thank for her escape. She had quickly turned her tail on the continent and raced back to Barra Head.

But now, after sleep-torn nights, Ava was so distraught that she decided she must swim to the gyre of Corry. She rarely went at this time of year. Late autumn was the time of her usual visit. It was an old mer ritual to take the white plaid to the sea cauldron and wash it, then spread it on the rocks of Hag's Head to dry on All Hallows' Eve. But a visit to the boiling, swirling waters of the gyre often soothed her mind. Had not her own mother sent her and Laurentia there when they were young stubborn girls— *"Go to Corry and give yourself to the gyre, then set yourself on the Hag's Head for a good think. That'll put some sense in you!"*

Well, it was time to go to Corry, set herself on the head of the Hag, and come back with some sense.

At the precise moment that Avalonia decided to swim to Corry, on the other side of the ocean Hepzibah Plum walked down to the beach for the first time in perhaps five years and flung the dead chick into the surf. Two women separated by three thousand miles of water on opposite shores, one human, one not quite.

A DECISION

THE NIGHTS HAD BEEN CLEAR, so May and Hugh had seen each other almost every evening for the better part of a week. On this particular night May leaned back and watched Hugh as he adjusted the scope. There was nothing she didn't love about him, from his eyes, to the way he twisted the telescope rings, to that soft exhalation of breath, the sigh that always accompanied the discovery of a new gift of the night in the changing heavens. "Say that poem by that fellow—not Shakespeare," May asked on this windless night as they drifted idly about the cove.

"What other fellow? There are several poets, you know."

"Yes, you know—the one about the fair-haired angel."

"Oh, William Blake's 'To the Evening Star.'"

"Yes, that one."

"Thou fair-hair'd angel of the evening,
Now, whilst the sun rests on the mountains,
*   light*
Thy bright torch of love; thy radiant crown
Put on, and smile upon our evening bed!
Smile on our loves, and while thou drawest the
Blue curtains of the sky, scatter thy silver dew
On every flower that shuts its sweet eyes
In timely sleep. Let thy west wind sleep on
The lake; speak silence with thy glimmering
*   eyes,*
And wash the dusk with silver. Soon, full soon,
Dost thou withdraw; then, the wolf rages wide,
And then the lion glares through the dun forest:
The fleeces of our flocks are cover'd with
Thy sacred dew: protect them with thine
*   influence!"*

When Hugh recited poetry there was something
in his voice, in the rhythm, that evoked within her

feelings similar to the ones she experienced when she swam. She could never tell him this, and it made her sad. For May, swimming was a kind of poetry. Within the currents, within the depths of the sea, the water had its rhythms and cadences that, once found, suffused her being with a quiet glory.

May picked up a piece of her hair and held it out. "I'm still not sure if red is considered fair hair."

"You're being awfully literal, May! A little poetic license can be used here." He paused. "And of course you fit the angel part, no quibbles there."

She smiled into the darkness. She liked being compared to an angel. An angel had wings, not a tail! An angel, in May's mind, was more than human. An angel was a spirit of the invisible world.

Since the dance, Hugh and May met not only for star watching but spent long hours together in the library, where May continued her study of trigonometry and together they pondered the Maury book. Their conversations about the influence of the stars on the currents transported May to another world. She forgot about Zeeba. Even her worries about finding her sisters faded away. But sometimes they veered too close to forbidden subjects. Just the previous after-noon she was suddenly struck by the oddity of Maury's phrase "the visible and the invisible ocean." She blurted out, "Don't you think it's odd, Hugh, that Maury calls the ocean, the real ocean, the visible one when there is so much we never see?"

"Like that lovely scallop comb you sometimes wear in your hair." He touched it. "Never seen a scallop like that. . . . What's wrong, May?"

Her face had turned pale, and her lower lip began to tremble. "Nothing! Nothing at all!"

"You look as if you've seen a ghost."

"No! No. I'm fine. Really." She changed the subject. "Why don't you take me sometime to the top of Abenaki so I can see the stars from there—the highest point." She wanted to distance herself as far as possible from the ocean.

"Would you really like that? Would your parents let you go?"

"Oh, yes." May shrugged. "My father has to take Zeeba to get new teeth down to Ellsworth."

"Zeeba? Zeeba's your mother, right?"

May was about to say no, she wasn't, but caught

herself. It would only bring her dangerously close again to a subject she was determined to avoid. "Yes, yes, she is," she replied firmly.

"Why do you call her Zeeba and not Mother?"

"Just do." She gave another shrug.

"Well, to get the best view of the stars we'd have to leave in the early evening and start to climb. It's not a hard climb. Nice path all the way, just some time involved."

They planned to go the following week, on the Tuesday that Gar was to take Hepzibah to Ellsworth.

Within that same week at least four other people came up to May and told her about the new serving girl over at Gladrock who was her spitting image. May could not help but wonder about this girl now. She was fearful. They might look alike but were they alike? Was the other girl less than human, too? And then again May wondered anxiously that if Hugh met the other girl he might like her better. What would it mean for May? She need not ask the question—the answer was all too clear. *It would mean I am truly a freak—a freak who is completely alone in this world.*

It was this anxiety that drove May to make a decision. She simply had to see this Hannah for herself. Perhaps a glimpse would be enough to know if in fact she had kin in this world. She would not, however, go right up to her. She would devise a way to see her but not be seen.

THE DEEP YEARNING

"WHOOO — EEE! IT'S COLD THIS MORNING!" the little girl shrieked as she waded into the water. "Oh, I forgot my swimming booties. Oh, well. Now, you count to three, Hannah, and then I'll plunge in."

May stood behind the thick fringe of the spruce trees that edged the cove of Gladrock. What struck her about the girl called Hannah, who was evidently taking care of the Hawleys' young child, was the fierce yearning she contained. It was something about the way Hannah stood at the very edge of the beach and seemed to strain forward as she looked out of the cove toward the open sea. May recognized the posture. It was exactly the way she had stood perched on the east side of Egg Rock, looking out to sea, ever since she could remember. There was an almost palpable longing, a longing that May had felt herself before she had crossed that border from one world into the other. A deep thrill coursed through her. She wanted to run toward the beach and embrace the girl, and yet instinctively she knew that she must not reveal herself. Although this girl was undoubtedly her sister, May knew she must avoid her until she, too, had crossed over. May thought of the words from the Bible, "To everything there is a season, and a time to every purpose under heaven: a time to be born and a time to die."

This was not Hannah's season, at least not yet. But how long would May have to wait?

May retreated into the deeper shadows of the woods. She would be patient.

A quarter of an hour later May was getting into the skiff at the dock when Rudd came up to her. *Oh, no*, she thought. If she had only been a little quicker, she would have been in the water already.

"Want me to cast you off?" he asked, taking the painter, which had been looped around the post, in his hand. May had the uneasy feeling that he had been watching her, waiting for this moment.

"Thank you, that would be nice," May answered, as politely as possible.

He undid the loop but kept it in his hand and crouched down.

"Well, are you or aren't you going to let me go?" she asked.

Rudd smiled and squinted one eye as if he were thinking about it. He wrapped a length of rope around his hand and pulled the skiff closer to the dock. *This is his game*, May thought. *He likes being in control.* But she vowed she would stay cool.

"Still mad at me?" he asked.

"I suppose so, until you apologize for your behavior."

"Behavior!" He pulled his head back and turned down the corners of his mouth in an expression of mock surprise. "Haven't had anybody talk about my behavior since I was in kindergarten. You think I'm a bad boy?"

"I think you're a rude man," May said. "Now, please let go of the rope."

He stood up and lazily twirled the painter in his hand. "Still seeing that Harvard boy?"

"It's not your business," May replied evenly, though she was almost gritting her teeth.

"Well, maybe only a strange fellow from away would fancy your kind."

My kind? May felt something jerk inside her.

Rudd simply threw the rope he was holding into the water, not bothering to coil it and drop it neatly onto the bow. May would have to walk forward and retrieve it, an awkward task when she was the only person on the boat, but she was trembling. *My kind? What does he mean? What does he know?*

"Hey, May," he called out. "They say there's a scullery girl up at Gladrock that's your spitting image but prettier. Think I'll ask her to the next dance."

May felt as if the wind had been knocked out of her. She couldn't catch her breath. It was not anger that flooded through her, but fear. Fear for the girl named Hannah. Fear for herself, for May realized that with Rudd, one was either predator or prey. Both she and Hannah would be vulnerable to the lurking brutality she had glimpsed in that vacant space behind his eyes.

26

A STAR-SPIKED NIGHT

THE TRAIL UP MOUNT ABENAKI was a steep one. The trees had begun to thin out as May and Hugh neared the summit, and the air cooled as the sun slipped swiftly toward the horizon.

"My goodness, May, every time I look back you're right on my heels. You don't tire, do you? You're not even panting! I've never met such a girl."

May felt the blood drain from her face.

"May, something wrong? You suddenly look awfully pale."

This was her chance to redeem herself. To hike like a normal girl. "Perhaps I took that last uphill a bit fast. I'll sit for a second."

"It's just a few more minutes to the peak. No need to rush."

She had actually been holding herself back so she would not pass Hugh on the mountain trail. Perhaps it was her swimming, but she realized that she rarely ran out of breath hiking or when she was underwater. She could swim for extended periods of time without surfacing. She even had more endurance than the two dolphins who sought her out to play.

She and Hugh had been hiking for almost two hours up Mount Abenaki. The stars were just rising, and silvery moths fluttered through the night. She had packed a picnic for when they got there.

"A moonlight picnic," Hugh had exclaimed. "Except no moonlight tonight. That's why it will be so spectacular for star watching."

They spread the cloth on a mossy rock ledge, and May began to unpack the deviled eggs and the sandwiches. There were also berries, cookies, and a jug of lemonade.

"Oh, dear!" May said. "Most of the berries fell out of the container and got squashed."

Hugh came over and looked into the basket. He picked up one raspberry. "Well, we'll just have to share what's left!" He put the berry between his lips and leaned toward May. She giggled and then pressed her mouth against his.

"Ummm!" Hugh sighed, then pulled himself back. "I think we'll have to try that again. I don't mean to suggest that you're greedy, May Plum, but you got the lion's share of that one. Let's be a little more fair next time."

"Halfsies?" she replied.

"Yes, that will take a lot of precision work dividing a raspberry exactly in half. Much practice needed."

He reached into the basket and retrieved another berry.

⚜   ⚜   ⚜

Thirty minutes later May peered into Hugh's berry-stained face. "We haven't eaten the deviled eggs yet."

"Who needs deviled eggs when there's May with raspberry sauce? You should see your face."

"You should see yours!" May replied. "Aren't we supposed to be watching the stars?"

He brought his face close to hers and looked into her eyes. "Yes. When you tip your head up I can see them reflected in your eyes."

"No, you can't!" May laughed.

"Yes, I can." He pressed himself closer to her. "I can see Vega and Altair and I can almost see . . ." He pulled back. May was somewhat relieved. She wanted him close, so close, but she was never sure when to stop. And did she really want him to stop? She broke from his embrace and quickly walked a few paces away. He came up behind her. "Are you cold?"

She was about to say she seldom got cold, but in fact she realized that she was a bit. The air felt colder to her than the water. "A little."

"Here, take my jacket." He wrapped it around her.

"I have to get back soon to tend the light. I mean, the clockworks are wound, but I set the light on a bit early, before it was dark, when we left. We really aren't supposed to burn the lamp during the day. Too much kerosene, you know. The lighthouse service makes us keep an exact accounting. I'll just have to say I spilled some by accident." She was not sure why she was rattling on so.

"Look up there! Now. Come on over to where I set the scope up. You'll see some great beauties." She looked straight up and saw the Milky Way stretched like a cobweb across the great black bowl of the sky.

"Look, there is Albireo," Hugh said. "See that point of very white light? Now come over to the telescope and look at the same point, and you'll see even more."

May was getting better at looking through the scope. It was a lot easier on solid ground instead of from the boat.

"See it?" he asked.

"I see something, but it doesn't look at all the same. It's like two — two —"

"Exactly — two suns. A double jewel. Many times more luminous than our own sun."

Our own sun; the words struck her oddly. It was as if she and Hugh owned the sky. And yet it seemed if anything the reverse. The stars owned the universe. She picked out some more of the familiar summer constellations she had learned about from Hugh, then took a step back and turned toward him.

"Matthew Fontaine Maury should not have called the sky the invisible ocean."

"What should he have called it, May?" Hugh asked. His lovely gray eyes had a deep solemnity to them.

"The silent world." She gave a shiver and thought of the sea and the symphony of watery sounds.

"Does it disturb you?"

"If it did, I doubt there is much I could do about it." May laughed, but her laughter sounded slightly anxious. "It's just . . ." She hesitated. "I'm not sure how to explain it, and who knows—perhaps there are galaxies beyond our own. But these stars and constellations have been turning and turning in this sublime silence and yet . . ."

". . . and yet they are indifferent." Hugh completed her thought.

"Yes, exactly! You understand. They are hugely indifferent toward us. Sounds silly, doesn't it? As if I am expecting attention from something a million miles away."

"Maybe it's why God made humans—to love in the colossal silence and star-spiked indifference of the universe."

That word again—*human*. Would her world of the sea seem as distant and silent to Hugh as these stars turning in the invisible ocean of air and sky seemed to her? Her secret life was more unknowable than the light of the most distant stars. Would he love her if he knew who she really was?

HARD QUESTIONS

JULY SLIPPED INTO AUGUST. May tried to go the back way out of the village whenever possible, through the thick woods that cloaked the point where Gladrock "cottage" rose like an immense gray-shingled, turreted hulk surrounded by rolling green lawns and lavish gardens. Screened by the dense stand of spruce, May observed Hannah on the beach with the spritely Ettie Hawley. She felt compelled to keep an eye on the scullery maid.

It had become almost a vigil with May; she wanted to know—and she felt sure she would know—instantly when Hannah had crossed over. But each time she came, she could tell by Hannah's strained posture that she was still filled with an unsatiated yearning for the sea. *It must be torture for her,* she thought, *having to watch little Ettie Hawley frolic in the sea.* Ettie was the only family member who seemed to put so much as a toe in the water. May enjoyed watching the child, for she had a saucy charm and wit that seemed unusual for such a sheltered little girl. Most of the summer people's children could hardly be considered children at all. They seemed more like miniature versions of their parents.

May had been in Bee's general store one day when two sallow little creatures came in with their nanny. Bee's had a wonderful supply of penny candy, but May herself had just bought the last few chocolate drops. The children were disappointed. So May took several from her own bag and offered them to the two youngsters. The little boy, who could not have been more than nine, looked up at her solemnly. "We cannot accept candy from natives, nor speak with them unless they are our servants." May snatched back her hand in shock. "I'm sure you understand," he said.

May crouched down and looked the pompous little boy straight on. "No, I don't understand at all. But I feel very sorry for you." Confusion swam in the child's eyes.

But May was sure that Ettie Hawley would not be that way. She not only lacked the inhibitions of these puffed-up, overbearing little brats, but she had a kind of inner grace mixed with a gentle humor. May enjoyed observing Ettie and Hannah together, and she hated to think of herself as spying upon them. But May also had an aching empathy for Hannah's keen yearning for the sea. There was no sign that Hannah Albury, for she had learned the girl's last name, had crossed over.

It was indescribably frustrating to May. It preoccupied her waking hours, even when she was with Hugh. She was so close to locating the *Resolute*, but Hannah seemed farther away than ever.

"May, I don't think you've heard a single thing I've said about these trigonometric functions in the last five minutes." They were in the library and Hugh had been helping her learn advanced trigonometry. May's recent research had revealed that the wreck had drifted either in a southwesterly or a northeasterly direction depending on the combination of currents and wind, which meant that it was either near Nantucket Shoals or Georges Bank. Once she knew this, she could go back to Maury and study the current diagrams and truly focus in on a likely location within a single region.

"Oh, I am so sorry. Yes. I know I've been distracted."

"Is it something at home?" May knew Hugh found it odd that she never spoke about her family. She had once described them as "queer folk" he wouldn't understand. Whenever he asked questions, May tried to change the subject, but she could sense Hugh growing suspicious. "Why do you even want to learn trigonometry, May? I've never actually understood your interest in Maury."

"I told you the first day I met you. I'm interested in currents," she replied.

"Ah, yes, the shipwreck off Egg Rock last winter. But it seems more than that to me."

"Does it now!" she shot back. She felt a panic rising within her.

"May!" Hugh was taken aback by the tone of her voice.

She knew she had gone too far, but she couldn't help it. "Look, there are certain things I—I just can't explain, that you can't ask me about. I'm sure you have things, too, that I shouldn't ask you about."

"Nothing, May, absolutely nothing." His face was crestfallen. There was no trace of those wonderful creases that normally bracketed his smiling eyes.

May felt terrible.

She looked up at him. There was a graveness in his expression that she had never seen before. May pressed her lips together. She would tell him a little, just a bit, but nothing about her secret life. "Not just that wreck—I am very interested in a shipwreck that happened fifteen, almost sixteen years ago. It was off of Georges Bank."

Hugh raised an eyebrow, and his wonderful smile threatened to break across his face. His next remark gave her a delightful out.

"And you think there is gold to be found?"

"Yes!" she replied gleefully, grateful for the escape. "And with it we can run away, and I'll be so rich I can build you an observatory just like the one at Harvard."

He laughed. "But tell me now, really, why are you so interested?"

May looked down at her hands. "I just am," she said simply. "And I am interested in how currents and drift could perhaps have affected it."

"How did you find out about this wreck?"

"I found a newspaper clipping someplace."

"What's the name of the ship?"

"HMS *Resolute*."

"Would you like me to look into it when I go down to Boston next week?"

May was taken aback. It was, of course, very generous of him, but it was frightening, too. It would put him in a position of possibly finding out more than she wanted him to know. She wasn't sure how to handle this.

"Well . . . ," she said slowly. "I—I'm not sure it's such a good idea, really."

Hugh blinked and looked at her hard. "May,

what is it?" He paused and gave a rather mirthless chuckle. "Don't tell me you're one of those covetous scholars who hoards information so you can claim all the glory."

"Don't make fun of me. I'd just rather do this myself."

"Rather do it yourself," he repeated abstractly.

"Yes, in my own way."

"You never even thanked me for offering, May."

"I'm—I'm sorry. Thank you. It was very kind of you. I was just surprised, that's all."

"Surprised that someone who really cares about you offered to help you with your secret research? What is the secret, May?" An edge was creeping into his voice.

She realized she would have to tell him something. If she didn't it would only make things worse. The secret would loom too large in his mind. She sighed. "I can tell you what little I already know."

"And what is that?"

May proceeded to tell him the longitude and latitude where the letter from the Newport Revenue

Cutter Service had reported finding drifting wreck-age, and that the captain was Walter Lawrence.

"I suppose I could take an extra day to go down to Newport on my next trip to Boston and talk to the people at the station there."

May seemed not to hear him.

"May!" he blurted out. "Sometimes it feels as if you're not even here."

"Whatever do you mean? I'm right here in front of you, silly." Her tone maddened him.

"But you're keeping things from me. If—if—" he stammered. She had never heard Hugh stammer in the time she had known him. "If there is someone else, I'll—I'll try to understand."

"Someone else! There is no one else." She inhaled sharply. "Not—not really." She was the one stammer-ing now. There *was* someone else. There was Hannah, and she knew there was another sister. But it was not the same thing. They were sisters, not boyfriends. Not like Hugh. It wasn't romantic. How could he say such a thing?

"Not really? Now, what the devil do you mean by

that? You're considering? Hedging your bets?" The blade of his sarcasm ripped through her.

May's mouth dropped open. She couldn't stand this. "That is hateful! I'm leaving right now."

"May! May!" he protested. "I am not hateful. I am not!" There was not a trace of the sarcasm. "May! May! I am sorry I spoke that way."

Her face turned stormy, and her green eyes glittered fiercely. "Well, I'm not sorry you did. Now I know who you really are."

He appeared suddenly very weary. He looked straight at May. "But, May, that's the problem exactly. I don't think I know who *you* are."

Her face turned chalky white—whiter than the moon. "I'm going back. Going back right this minute." She ignored the sadness and confusion on his face and left.

"I hear'd them folks up at Gladrock have hired a whole orchestra from New York City to come up and play for their picture party."

"A pastry chef, too. Pearl Haskell says that the regular cook is in a dither over that. Feels she can make cakes as good as any Frenchie from New York."

One could not walk through the village of Bar Harbor these days without hearing about the ball that was to be held at Gladrock, the estate of the Hawley family. The party was planned in celebration of the unveiling of a portrait that had been painted by the renowned artist Stannish Whitman Wheeler. That was how May found out the name of the man who had come up to her in the lane that day. There was other talk, too, concerning the party, or rather one of the Hawley daughters, a girl name Lila, who was said to have a delicate temperament. Or as May heard one day when she was in Bee's, "Downright loony is what she is!"

"Yep, she just got out of the loony bin," spoke up another lobsterman, in high rubber boots, who had come in.

"Sanitarium," Mrs. Bee said from behind the counter. She didn't like people gossiping about the summer folk. It wasn't good for business. They could gossip all they wanted to during the winter but not in the summertime, during high season.

"Loony bin," muttered the lobsterman, sliding his eyes away from Mrs. Bee.

"IT'S HAPPENED!"

THE NEXT DAY May took Hepzibah into the village for an appointment with Dr. Holmes. May was still reeling from her fight with Hugh. She regretted what she had said and she wondered if she had driven Hugh off for good.

When they went into the doctor's office, his wife greeted them with an agitated expression.

"I am so sorry, Mrs. Plum, but Doctor Holmes was called away on an emergency over at Gladrock." Fear leaped up in May.

"Oh—oh, I hope—" she stammered. "I hope it's nothing with that lovely little girl, Ettie."

"No, it's an unfortunate situation with the eldest daughter. I believe her name is Lila."

"Well, do you know when this 'unfortunate situation' will be fixed?" Hepzibah snapped.

"It's an emergency, Mother." It was the first time in months that May had called Zeeba Mother.

"But I've come all the way in here. I don't leave Egg Rock much. I'm not up to it."

"Well, you are welcome to stay here as long as you like and wait for Doctor Holmes to return."

Hepzibah gave a little sniff. "Thank you." She set herself down on the oak bench. "Might you fetch me a pillow for my back? This bench is rather hard. And perhaps a cup of tea? It might settle my stomach. That's why I'm here."

As soon as Mrs. Holmes left the room, May turned and looked coldly at Hepzibah. "I'm going out for a bit. I'll be back."

"Suit yourself."

May headed directly for Gladrock, but as she walked through the village she heard other news. "It ain't just the crazy girl. They say one of the servants done disappeared as well."

"What? What's that?" May stopped short by the post office.

"Oh, hello, May." It was Carrie Welles, wife of the postmaster and also probably the snoopiest woman in the village. She feasted on gossip. And if gossip could make one plump it had done so for Carrie Welles. She was perfectly round. One got the impression that if bumped, she might roll down the street right into the harbor. "Yes, that servant girl who everyone says is the spitting image of you. She got into some kind of tussle with the eldest daughter, Lila. And they say she just took off."

"But where did she take off to?"

Carrie shrugged her plump shoulders. Her double chin quivered. "Who's to know?"

"I done heard they sent Captain Eaton out in the motor launch for her," Thad Roberts said as he walked by.

"A boat!" May gasped. "They think she went—" Before she could finish the sentence she began running toward Gladrock. *Could it be true? Could it have happened? Has Hannah finally crossed over?*

This time May stood in the shadows of dark pines that edged the driveway witnessing a strange and eerie tableau. A black city carriage stood in front under the porte cochere of the house. She saw two figures dressed in white nurse uniforms walking on either side of a young woman who appeared to be in a trance. She caught sight of Dr. Holmes just behind the trio and, to one side, Ettie stood next to a girl whom May assumed to be her sister. Suddenly she saw Ettie wrench free from the group. "Hannah!" she screamed, and darted across the lawn.

May heard a crackle in the woods, and not twenty yards from her Hannah Albury, May's sister, stepped out of the trees. Neither one had seen the other through the dense boughs of the dark pines. The little girl ran to embrace Hannah. Hannah turned her head toward the ocean, which was obscured now by the trees. Her face was a landscape of devastation and grief at what she had left behind. It only took one look for May to know that, at last, her sister had crossed the border. All May could think was, *It's happened! At last it's happened.* And she was joyous.

"I AM MAY!"

IT HAD BEEN THREE NIGHTS since Hannah had crossed, and May could not find her anywhere. She was growing desperate. Could she have been mistaken? A terrible thought came to her. Could Rudd have done something? Hadn't he said that he was going to go up to Gladrock and see the scullery girl who was prettier than she was?

May had considered simply walking up to the Hawleys' house and asking to see Hannah. Or she might write her a note. But it didn't seem right. It went against some deeply rooted instinct. One did not go on land to seek out mer folk.

Two days later, when she was trimming the lighthouse wick, she heard her father on the steps coming up to the lantern room. He was back from a trip into the village.

"Barometer's dropping like a shot. At the post office the telegraph just came through from the weather station down round Portland that there's a storm intensifying off the Carolinas."

It didn't surprise May. There had been a heaviness in the air for a day or so. The wind gusted in an erratic manner. It felt as if she were being slapped by wet, warm rags. But May felt a deep thrill. She loved swimming in storms, the wilder the better. She had learned how to perch tail end on a steep wave to surf down its face on a long angle. She tried to ride each wave as far as possible, just under the curling edge, until the wave collapsed. She wondered if Hannah had learned to do this yet.

She supposed this storm would mean that Hugh would be delayed returning from Boston. *So much the better.* She was mortified every time she thought of their argument. She had actually screamed at him. She was thankful that Miss Lowe had not been there but had gone to the post office. And there was no guarantee that Hugh would return. Maybe he was done with her. She at least had Hannah to think about—a much more hopeful situation since Hannah had crossed over. True, having a sister was not like having a sweetheart, but at least with Hannah, when they finally met, there would be no secrets.

By the next afternoon the storm had become a hurricane and was moving up the east coast at a fearsome clip. May and her father spent the entire day rigging the hurricane shutters and making the lighthouse as secure as possible. Hepzibah moaned about how the dropping barometric pressure always provoked her complications. She had taken out her new false teeth and put them in a glass of water. "Soon as that barometer goes below twenty-nine my gums swell up on me."

But she could not get a speck of attention from either Gar or May because they were too busy. "May, if this things hits, I think we're going to say good-bye to those chickens unless we bring them in the house. Hurricane wind will just pick up those coops and fly them away."

"Can't we fit them in the storehouse between the kerosene kegs?"

"Maybe a few but not all."

"Okay. I'll start moving as many as I can there and bring the rest in here."

"Oh, mercy!" Hepzibah wailed. "That'll start up my asthma for sure."

"Well, what do you want me to do, woman?" Gar said with an uncustomary rancor in his voice that made May turn around. "Should we roast them all tonight?" May had never seen her father stand up to Hepzibah in quite this manner.

It caught Zeeba off guard and she blinked at her husband but recovered shortly. "Oh, you're such a card, Edgar Plum!" she snarled. "Polly must have loved your sense of humor."

Gar stopped midway out the door to nail a shutter for the parlor window. He smiled almost dreamily. "Matter of fact she did," he said softly.

May felt a deep twinge in her and then caught the hatred in Hepzibah's eyes.

This hurricane cannot come soon enough! May thought. She was desperate to get out into the wildness of it. To leave all this behind.

She knew that when the mercury in the glass of a barometer drops to below twenty-eight, the plunge in atmospheric pressure can induce a soporific effect in human beings, a deep drowsiness. But as the storm grew closer May felt a joyful agitation. She would be able to sneak out earlier than she ever had before.

She was not sure how long she had been riding the steep waves just south of Simon's Ledge. The ledge where Gar had found her was one of her favorite places to visit. She had often wondered what would have happened if he hadn't found her. Would she have died? Would the dolphins have taken care of her, nursed her with their own milk as they did their young? These ledges were, she felt, as true a home as any for her.

The currents no longer seemed so elusive to her. She felt them in her blood, in her bone. They were connections to her deepest and most visceral memories—a physical tie to her past. She closed her eyes and thought about the map in the library, focusing on the area around Nantucket Shoals and Georges Bank. She felt the rush of a current pass over her and suddenly everything snapped into place. It could never be Georges Bank—not with the way the current turned. It was Nantucket Shoals, of course. Had to be! It was as if she had always known this, swam this in her mind. She could even feel those currents pulsing through her now. She knew the currents in a way that Maury did not despite all his experiments of setting out drift buoys and his reading of thousands of pages of ships' logs. She knew that nothing Hugh could bring back from his trip to Boston and Newport would add to her ability to determine the location of the main part of the wreckage of the HMS *Resolute*. His information might give her a history of the ship and its captain, but she knew that she could find her way to the wreck. She just did not want to go alone. She had been waiting for Hannah. They should go together.

But how was she to find her? The eye of the storm was approaching. She could tell. It was somewhere between Simon's Ledge and Egg Rock. She was curious. She had heard of the calm at the eye of the storm. She dove deep and swam a short distance underwater. She could detect from the currents flowing over the flukes of her tail that she was closing in on the eye. She swam toward the surface and broke through into a pool of water as still as a pond on a windless summer day. There was such peace, an unimaginable peace. A sense of fulfillment, of—of—Her mind searched for the word. Of *connection*. It was in that moment she saw her.

"Hannah!" she cried out, and lifted her tail in the thin sliver of moonlight revealed by the eye of the storm. "Hannah! I am here. May! I am May—your sister!"

MY SISTER, MYSELF

As they swam toward each other, the green light of their eyes seemed to meld together. It was as if they were drawing nearer and nearer to the very source of their lives, and their sisterhood. They did not rush but moved through the water with a deliberate slowness as if to savor every second, each basking in the overwhelming realization that at last there was someone like her; rejoicing in the knowledge that they were no longer alone in the world. There were four words that streamed through both their minds like a song—*I am not alone!*—as they met up in the very center of the storm's eye and embraced each other for long minutes. Then May, cupping her mouth to Hannah's ear, said over the roar of the wind, "Follow me!" And the two girls together swam out of the eye of the hurricane.

Diving deeply to avoid the tumult of the storm-torn world above, May and Hannah swam side by side toward Simon's Ledge. At last one of the voids that had haunted May, that empty shape beside her, was truly filled. She felt an inexpressible happiness, a sense of near completion. Thoughts flowed between them without the need for actual words. Never had she felt so deeply understood. Often May and Hannah would glance at each other and smile joyfully in their bond. Their breathing synchronized, and they only had to surface two times for air. On their third rise they had arrived at Simon's Ledge.

"For me it began here, near these ledges," May said as the girls swam around the roots of Simon's Ledge. She suddenly started to laugh. "Do you realize we are talking underwater?"

Hannah blinked. "We are, aren't we!" The two girls reveled in this sudden realization. And May was aware that although she no longer experienced that almost crushing loneliness, there was still that tender place somewhere within her, that bruise she felt if she pressed on it, if she thought about Hugh. Did Hannah have such a bruise?

"I think I've sort of talked this way before but it was only with seals and dolphins and it wasn't exactly words."

"Yes, I know what you mean. All the time we were swimming out here I felt as if we were in some sort of wordless conversation, but now the words are clear."

May dove down a bit deeper and came up right under Hannah and looked her in the face. "Do you realize, Hannah, that until now I felt I was completely alone in the world, a freak—a freak of nature, a terrible mistake of some sort—but now—now—"

"We aren't freaks. We're sisters!"

Sisters! Such a simple word and yet it seemed almost magical in its power—its power to banish the desolation that had lurked at the very center of their existences.

They were swimming side by side, and occasionally the flukes of their tails would brush up against each other.

"But what do you mean when you say it began here?" Hannah asked, turning to May.

May almost realized as soon as she said it that this was not quite accurate. It had begun long before Simon's Ledge. When they had climbed up on the ledge, she slipped the chain with the locket over her head. "I have to show you something." She unlocked the little hinge and opened the locket, cupping it in her hand to protect it from the wind. "See that?" she whispered.

"What is it?"

"It's a bit of my hair—my baby hair."

"How'd you get it?"

"I found it. Found it in a blanket in the sea chest— the sea chest from the HMS *Resolute*." She briefly told the story of the ship.

"So this—I am almost positive—is where Gar found me, floating in that sea chest from the *Resolute*, right here near Simon's Ledge."

"Who's Gar?" Hannah asked.

"My father . . . well, my foster father."

"And did he tell you what you were? That you were mer?"

"Oh, no!" May then proceeded to give her a short

history of how she was found—the wreck of the *Resolute*, and how she was determined to swim there. And now that she had found Hannah they could go together. She told her, too, about her life with Gar and Zeeba on Egg Rock.

"Oh, dear. It sounds—grim."

"Gar's nice. I love him. It would break his heart if he knew that I have come back to the sea. It's a problem, a painful problem."

"If you leave him he'll be left with that wife—Zeeba!"

"Yes," May replied quietly. She wasn't ready to tell Hannah quite yet about Hugh. Her connection with Hugh went much deeper than the one with Gar. She had done things on that mountain that she was not sure she could ever tell anybody—not even her own sister. "But it's your turn now. Tell me, where did you come from? Were you found?"

"Well, somebody found me. I'm not sure who. I was put in an orphanage, The Boston Home for Little Wanderers, and then when I turned fifteen they sent me off to work. I got this job in the Hawleys' house."

"Do you like it?"

"It's a long story."

"We have time."

"Yes, I suppose so." Hannah then began to tell her story—the terrible problems with Lila, who was thankfully now tucked away in some sort of hospital for the mentally ill; her own deep connection with little Ettie. When she had finished, she sighed. "And I guess that's it." Although she knew it wasn't. For she, like May, had purposely left out the part of her story about the painter Stannish Whitman Wheeler, not just her love for him and his for her, but the deep suspicion she had that he, too, was mer, or had been.

"There's more," May said softly.

Hannah looked at her in alarm. "I've told you everything I can."

"No, no. I believe you. There is more that I know about our story."

"What?"

"The ship that wrecked, our mother was on that ship."

"Our mother?"

"Yes, and our sister."

"Our sister?"

"Yes. There is a third mer baby that was lost that night." May briefly told about the carvings of three tiny mermaids on the chest.

"And this sister is still alive?"

May nodded solemnly. "I am sure, and she will come here."

It was not long until the dawn. May had to get back to the lighthouse, and Hannah knew she must return to Gladrock. There was no time for May to tell Hannah how together they could find the wreck. But they planned to meet the next night at the cave beneath the cliffs, where Hannah went to change her clothes before returning to Gladrock. May knew these cliffs, and she assured Hannah that she would find the cave easily. They hugged each other and swam away in different directions. And oddly enough one of the spaces beside May swam away as well. Yet she still felt almost complete for the first time in months, or perhaps ever.

High above the gyre of Corry, on the promontory of Hag's Head, Avalonia sat wrapped in her white plaid. She had visited the gyre and sat atop the head of the Hag almost every week throughout the summer, and every time her thoughts came a bit more clearly. She would sit a bit longer on Hag's Head, above the roiling waters of the gyre, and listen to those deepest ocean murmurs, open her mind to her sea roots and those ancient instincts that were known among mer folk as the Laws of Salt.

For grown mermen or -women the Laws of Salt were like scripture running through their veins. One just had to quiet one's self enough to listen well. Over the summer weeks she had done just this, and now she began to know that two of Laurentia's children lived, after all these years. Two lived and had found each other, somewhere far from here, far from the Hag's Head, across the sea.

THE COLDEST WORD

BY THE TIME **M**AY RETURNED to the lighthouse the worst of the hurricane had passed. A soft constant drizzle now fell. The air was still thick with clouds, and the sky hung heavy and gray. In such conditions, particularly after a big storm, the practice was to let the light burn longer into the morning. It was safe, however, to remove the chicken coops from the kitchen as well as those she had stashed in the storage shed. She then went to the larger shed, where they had put Bells Two for the storm.

"You can get out now, de-ah!" she said to the cow. Bells blinked back at her. "You survived the hurricane all right?" The cow flicked her tail as if shooing a fly away. "Don't think there are any flies left to bother you. They all blew away." May led her out and tethered her to the post, then fetched a stool and sat down with a pail to milk her.

For some reason May had a powerful appetite. She planned to make a big breakfast for them all. She only wished Hannah could sit down with them at the table. Wouldn't that give Zeeba a start! But she knew Gar would like Hannah.

The sun began to show weakly over the horizon. The sharp hiss of the milk spraying into the bucket and the crushing sound of the waves rolling in on the beach made a lovely music. *I can't believe it. I have a sister! I have a sister!* As soon as she got a chance she would get out the charts that Gar kept of the New England coast. When she met Hannah this evening she wanted to have it all planned out. The distance to Georges Bank was perhaps two hundred miles as the crow flew, but as the mer girl swam, the distance was slightly longer. But she knew that when she swam full power, she could exceed the speed of any steamer that plied the coastal waters. The days were shortening now, which meant the nights were growing longer. She felt that she and Hannah could make it down and back within the course of a single night. They had to go together, and soon. They could not wait for their third mer sister. The urgency was unbearable. They needed to find the wreck now!

"My, my, you're awfully cheery this morning," Hepzibah commented as she came into the kitchen. May stood in front of the big cast-iron stove, frying up onions in salt pork. She poured a pitcher of eggs she'd beaten up with the fresh milk.

"Yes, I'm feeling good. Bells survived the hurricane fine."

"And so did you, I see," Zeeba added. "Cows and girls," she muttered. May ignored the remark.

Gar came in from outside. "You already got the chickens sorted out. Thank you, de-ah. I would have helped you with that."

"Oh, it wasn't any problem, Pa. I was up early."

"Well, I don't think we suffered any damage here. Don't know how they fared in Bar Harbor. I'm sure some of those yachts must have torn loose from their moorings if they didn't take them over to the hole.

And that hole can't fit in all the new yachts they been building these days."

The hole was the hurricane hole near Otter Creek that was the safest place to take a boat during nasty weather. "When the chop goes down we could sail the skiff over and check up on things in the village. Lend a hand if anybody needs help," Gar added.

May looked at her father. He was such a kind man. How could he stand being married to Zeeba? She often caught herself wondering what Gar's life would have been like with another woman—not just Polly but anyone. There was one thing for sure. Ever since the time of the nor'easter those long months ago, Gar had not touched a drop of liquor. He seemed to have come into his own in a way that continued to surprise May. It was as if he were gathering a new strength deep inside himself, a new authority. But she knew that although he was better at standing up to Zeeba, he would never leave her.

Later that morning May and her father took the skiff to Bar Harbor. The town pier was half underwater from the storm surge, and lobster traps that had been stacked at the fish pier bobbled about freely now in the harbor, along with bait barrels.

"Raise up the centerboard, May, and we'll run her right up on the beach, since it looks like the only working pier is the fish one, and we better not take up any room."

The small crescent of beach was piled high with debris flung up from the hurricane: lobster pots, barrels, and dead fish, small ones—mackerel, stripers, smelts, herring—their eyes glazed and becoming filmy, their gills still open as if caught in a last gasp. She imagined them just hours before, flopping about, stunned at their sudden forced expulsion from the sea.

May turned to her father. "You want me to jump out with the painter and tie us up?" She saw a pulse start to work in Gar's jaw.

"Oh, no! No! I'll do it. I'm still limber enough." He gave a nervous laugh.

He's still worried, May thought, worried that she would instantly become something else lest the tiniest drop of water touch her foot, or God forbid, her jump was short and she fell in. Did he think she would be like one of those fish that hours before had been gasping on land? Did he know that she had crossed over and come back? Of course not. But how often would she come back—for Gar, for Hugh?

"Hi! Gar, May. Can I give you a hand with that painter?" May's stomach clutched. It was Rudd.

"Oh, Rudd, kind of you. May, get up there and toss him the painter."

May walked up to the bow grimly. She was sick of this man. Sick of his lurking about the edges of her life, sick of that festering brutality she detected in him. But most of all she was sick of her own fears of him. He preyed on weakness. She coiled the painter and flung it toward Rudd. He had to back away a bit, for she had aimed for his face.

"Gotcha on the end of a line again, darlin'," he said in a low voice that only May could hear. He tethered the rope to a granite block on the beach. May jumped quickly onto a pile of seaweed.

"She's nimble, that one," Gar said as he swung a leg over the bow.

"Oh, quite the mountaineer, I think!" May's blood froze. *No, he couldn't have!* Was it possible that he had followed her and Hugh that day? Would he have seen them that night? "Yep, she moves fast, that one!"

May's face turned as red as her hair. "I'm going to the library to see if Miss Lowe's all right."

"Library's fine, May. You can still go there and read your books with the doctor or that Harvard fellow."

May tipped her head. "Why do you say these things?"

"What things, May? What things are you talking about?"

"I read in the library. I take out books, and what I read and who I talk to while I am there is my business."

"That so?" He said it so smugly. Then a smile crawled across his face. And very casually he said, "Post office needs some help. I even got a letter here for you."

"For me?" May bit her lip slightly. Why did he keep smiling at her? It was unnerving.

"Yep, all the way from Boston."

"Why do you have it?"

"Well, when Carrie Welles saw that I was heading over toward your skiff she just handed it to me. She said everything's at sixes and sevens. Only a few letters didn't get drenched. So here's yours." He reached into his pocket and handed it to her.

May willed herself not to look at the envelope. She took it and immediately put it in her pocket and walked away stiffly in the direction of the library. "See you in a bit, May," her father called. She did not reply.

The library was fine, and once she had said hello and made polite chitchat with Miss Lowe she went to the window seat in the back corner, where she had first read the book of Matthew Fontaine Maury. She sat down and tore open the envelope.

Her heart sank as she saw the tiny piece of newsprint with a small headline: BRITISH SHIP OF THE LINE SINKS: ALL FEARED LOST.

Dear May,

My research did not yield much. This small clipping was all I could find. My

return to Bar Harbor has been delayed
because of some research that Professor
Healy has asked me to do.

But he is returning, May thought. *He is coming back.* But with the next sentence her heart sank once more.

Perhaps this information might help
you find what you are looking for.
Cordially,
Hugh Fitzsimmons

Cordially! The word was like a slap across her face. It resounded like a clap of thunder in her head. *Cordially*—it was the coldest word in the English language.

FASTER THAN AN EAGLE?

THEY WERE PERCHED ON A SLANTED ROCK in the cave at Otter Creek. It was the perfect hideaway and May found it completely charming. Lovely mosses and lichen filigreed its walls. The water lapped in, but there were dry places as well to store clothes and even tins of food that Hannah had brought from the Gladrock kitchen. They were eating molasses cookies.

"You see, Hannah, I think if we can find this wreck we can find out where we came from, and— and . . ." She hesitated, for it seemed wrong to raise false hope. "And find out if there are others like us."

"You really think there are others? Could be others?" Hannah asked.

"I am sure that we have another sister. I think we are destined to find her as we seemed destined to find each other."

"Maybe she will come to us, as I came here to you."

"Maybe, but maybe she won't, and what about our parents?" May asked.

"They most likely died in the shipwreck, don't you think?"

"But who were they?" There was an urgency in May's voice.

"Yes, who were they?" Hannah said softly. "All these years I thought I came from nowhere, really. When other girls at the orphanage would daydream about their parents—oh, how they daydreamed—I never uttered a word because I dared not dream. Imagine if I had said my mum was a mermaid or my father a merman. They would have shipped me off like Miss Lila to the loony bin."

"Never mind what other people think. I know how to find this ship. There's a current we can catch. It's off Grand Manan. We have to go a little bit out of our way to catch it, but it's worth it."

May bit into one of the cookies Hannah had brought as she conjured up that stream of water that flowed south. "These cookies are wonderful, by the way."

"Mrs. Bletchley is the best cook."

"And she doesn't mind you taking food?"

"Oh, no. She's always pressing snacks on us."

"What's it like being in rich people's houses?"

"It's complicated," Hannah said.

"Complicated how?"

"We all have to know our place. Mr. Marston has a whole chart that explains who's where in the order of things and what our jobs are."

"Are they nice, though—the Hawleys—except for that girl you told me about, the crazy daughter?"

"I don't know. I mean, people at my level in service never really talk with them that much. We're not supposed to. Except, of course, for Ettie. She talks to anybody or anything. She'll talk to a tree."

"No!"

"Yes. I caught her, one day, talking away as if this spruce were a person—saying it should grow some limbs lower down so she could climb up easier." Both girls burst out laughing. "Ettie is a character, and she makes her own rules. But tell me more about this current you discovered."

"Well, I think it spins off from the Gulf Stream. It will boost our speed by twice, at least, maybe even three times."

"How fast can we go in the current—as fast as the *Prouty*?" Hannah asked. May cocked her head and looked at Hannah with surprise. "Why are you looking at me like that, May Plum?" Hannah asked, and bit into her cookie.

May had to remember that Hannah had only been swimming a few days. She didn't really know her own power. "Hannah, we can already go that fast!"

"We can?"

"I've tested it."

"You have?"

"Yes." May told her about when she had gone out nearly to Nova Scotia and came back racing an eagle.

"It's this," May said when she finished the story,

and flipped the flukes of her tail up from the water. "All our power comes from our tails. Amazing, isn't it, that our two spindly legs could change into something so powerful?"

"So now tell me more about the *Resolute*."

"Well, I've had this plan from when I first went into the closet where the sea chest was. I think the next step in the plan, now that I found you, is to go to the *Resolute*. I think I could have done it by myself but . . . well . . ." She reached out her hand and took Hannah's. "I didn't want to go alone."

"I understand," Hannah said. "I wouldn't have wanted to, either."

May smiled. It felt so good to be understood completely. She continued explaining about the steps of the plan that had come to her when she found out that Zeeba and Gar were not her parents. "It was a horrible moment in so many ways when Zeeba came out with that. But it was good, too. It freed me.

"I told you how I figured out that I was found in the sea chest and that Gar had hidden it away in this little closet up in the service area to the lantern room? It's not like I had never noticed the closet before, but I had just never thought about it. I can't explain, but I sensed that if I could get into that little closet there was something in it connected to me."

"Well, you were surely right about that."

"The thing I can't figure out is why I was found in it and not you and—and—"

"Our other sister," Hannah said.

"Yes. Wouldn't it have made sense to put us all in one sea chest?"

"Maybe it started to leak. Maybe the three of us weighed too much and they had to put us in something else."

May's eyes brightened. "Heavens! I never thought of that. That would make perfect sense, of course. And then we floated away in different directions— me to Maine, you to Boston?"

"I guess."

"What do you mean, you guess? Isn't that where the orphanage, The Home for Little Wanderers, is? You wandered to Boston, or floated there."

"I suppose. But where did the third baby go? You're absolutely sure there is a third?"

"Yes, absolutely. I feel her," May said firmly.

"But how can you feel something that's not there?"

"The way I felt you before you came to Bar Harbor, before you crossed over." May paused. She swept her hand slowly down her side. "You were like a space here, a shape beside me but empty. And then after we met the emptiness swam away because you were here." She reached out and touched Hannah's hand.

Hannah had grown very still. "I think I know what you mean. There has been something pressing just lightly against my sides ever since I came to Gladrock. Now this side feels fine." She touched the right side of her rib cage. "But there is something still there on this side." She made a cradling gesture with her left arm.

"It's her," May said quietly. "She'll come. I know it. But we don't have to wait for her. We can swim to the *Resolute* soon. So that by the time she comes we might know more." May looked around the cave. "I like this place. I like it so much. It can be like our little house."

"I always dreamed of a little cottage by the sea. When Mrs. Larkin, at the orphanage, asked me what I would do with the money I earned from working in service to a fine family, I told her that I would buy a cottage by the sea. But this is much better, isn't it?"

"Much."

"I wonder, though, would it be too cold in winter? Could we even swim in winter?"

"When I crossed over it wasn't summer. And we'd had very cold weather, but I didn't really feel it that much. It's odd, but I rarely feel cold." Her mind flashed back to the night on Mount Abenaki. In the deepest part of the night Hugh's teeth had almost been chattering. For it was cold on that mountaintop, and yet it hadn't really bothered May that much. She stopped herself from thinking about that night. She couldn't anymore. The word—that loathsome word *cordially*—rang in her brain, not like a thunderstorm but rather a doleful tolling. She focused on Hannah instead. "So two nights from now we'll meet here and set out for the *Resolute*."

"Yes, May. Oh, yes!"

May left and Hannah watched her swim off. Hannah, too, had thoughts she wanted to push from her mind. She recalled her last meeting with the painter Stannish Whitman Wheeler. She knew she loved him deeply. She thought he loved her. Dare she ever tell May that she not just suspected but really knew that he was mer as well, or rather had been? Her last meeting with him had been so frightening. He knew she had crossed over. His words rang in her ears as if he were in front of her in the cave.

"Listen to me, Hannah!" he had said. *"Right now you can go back and forth between two worlds. But it will not be this way always. In a year, at the very longest, you must make a choice. You must be of one world or the other!"* And then when she refused to believe him he had said, *"It is true. I am living proof. You can never go back!"*

THE HMS *RESOLUTE*

IT'S LIKE TRAVELING through a starry night made of *water, not air*, May thought. The phosphorescence of the water spun by them like galaxies. There were times they were swimming so fast that May felt as if her body were sliding out ahead of her mind. The current swept them through the night sea, and when they broke through the surface and leaped high to catch a gulp of air even the wind was with them and pushed them farther until they dove back down to that starry river.

"We're getting closer," May said.

"Already?" Hannah asked.

"I told you it would be fast. Now we're going to have to swim out of the current or we'll be swept by."

As they swam from the current it felt as if the whole world had slowed.

May might have thought that it was the charts and Maury's book combined with her own instinct for currents that had guided her this far. And in part that was true. But now another guidance system that had nothing to do with reckoning was set into motion. It was the Laws of Salt. Independent of any compass, it pulled one toward the long-lost shadows of kin.

They were very near. May felt it, and soon Hannah felt it as well. They barely needed to speak as they slipped through the water. Angling their flukes slightly this way or that they honed in on the sea grounds of the wreck. Soon a shape rose from the grassy seafloor. The HMS *Resolute*. Its hull loomed like a ghostly vision. Although logically they knew it could no longer sail, it seemed driven by a spectral wind. A large halibut, with its strangely skewed face in which the eyes seemed to slide off to one side, swam out of a gaping hole in the bow. The dark portholes emerged like the sockets in a dead man's skull, and yet there was a strange beauty to the ship.

Both May and Hannah put on a tremendous burst of speed.

But they suddenly stopped short in the water, and twining their tails around each other they locked arms. For the first time they shivered. But it was not with cold. A face drifted above them — a face just like theirs.

"It's — it's . . ." Hannah could not complete the thought.

"Our mother," May said, swimming up toward the figurehead that extended from the bow. Although most of the paint had long worn away the features were unmistakable. They both touched their chins at the same time and felt the slight dimple in the middle. The cheekbones were rounded and high like theirs and the mouth had the same generous lower lip and delicately bowed upper one. Her neck curved down to her shoulders, and the artist who had carved the figurehead had modestly let tendrils of her hair cover her breasts. But her midriff was bare and just beneath her navel, where her pelvis began, were finely carved scales. May had seen figureheads on the ships that plied the coastal waters all her life. They were most often of women, sometimes of men— usually kings or military heroes and sometimes gods. But this face was instantly recognizable to May and Hannah, for it was so similar to their own faces.

The girls entwined themselves around her, caressing her hair, brushing the hardwood curves of her face, her neck, her lovely shoulders. Did they imagine that she heard their voices, felt their tears, their kisses, their longing? That her wooden eyes gazed down on them and saw them? There was a strange mingling of joy and profound sorrow. They had found what they had lost. The figurehead was the connection they had longed for, but the broken hull of the ship hovered over them like the shadow of an ultimate disconnection and all that could never be recovered.

Despite years of being polished by the ocean there were still vague traces of paint on the figurehead's face. The deep green of her eyes, the brilliant red hair, the flush on her cheeks, and the ripe rosiness of her lips. Their hearts were broken, and yet they felt a mending taking place within the deepest part of their beings. They belonged to her. They had been born of this woman. They were her daughters. And for now that was all they needed to know.

They swam through the interior of the hull. In the aft cabin, which was mostly destroyed, they found an overturned navigation desk. This must be the captain's quarters. "Look, a comb like yours!" Hannah said, picking up a scallop shell that was in a half-open drawer of the desk. "It must have been hers."

"Take it, Hannah, you should have it."

"Oh, that's so sweet of you."

"I already have one. Don't be silly." But in truth she did want something of her mother's. She wondered if she could find anything, just any little thing.

She swam over what must have been a bed. There were little cubbyholes above the head of the bed where things could be stored. She reached into the first one and found a chambered nautilus. The creature inside did not take kindly to being disturbed. The next cubbyhole was blocked by a starfish. But in the third one she saw what appeared to be a flattish rock propped up. It was wedged in tightly and it took her a good deal of time to dislodge it.

"What is it, May?" Hannah said, swimming over.

"I'm not sure." May replied.

"It looks broken."

"Yes, it does. But look at that feathery design on it. Like a lily."

"Do you think it belonged to our mother? It's so pretty. Maybe it was a keepsake of hers."

May looked up for a moment as the shafts of silver light from a full August moon illuminated the beautiful design on the ancient rock. "Yes, a keepsake. I'm sure!" May said, and smiled at Hannah. "It's our mother's."

WHITE SQUALL

MAY KNEW THAT HUGH must have returned by this time, but so far she had not heard a word from him. She tortured herself with visions of him dancing at the fancy parties of the summer people. Again the word *cordially* ran through her brain. How could he have said that to her, after their night on Mount Abenaki? The more she thought about it, the more tarnished the memories became. She was caught between terrible anger and deep regret.

She loved Hannah, but love for a sister was different from the love she had or thought she had with Hugh. How could he have been so hurtful? Hugh's coldness cut deeper than anything Rudd had ever done.

The question May kept asking herself was that although she had found part of her family would she ever have one of her own—have children, a husband? She had found the sea, but was increasingly certain she had lost everything else.

Later that afternoon, May was up in the lantern room trimming the wick of the lamp, when she began to hear the slap of the wind around the eaves of the roof and saw the railing on the circular deck outside the lantern room shake. She looked out. She found the clear sky alarming. There was not a cloud in it. She went to the window, and the water was being whipped to a froth. Then May let out a small yelp.

"What in the name?" Hugh! Hugh's boat was heading toward Egg Rock.

No! Dread welled up within her. Suddenly there was a demonic whistling sound, and the windows of the lantern room began to shiver. She watched transfixed as the small sailboat heeled so its spars were parallel to the sea. *He has too much sail up!*

There was a haunting familiarity that flooded through her. Six months before she had stood clinging to the piling on their dock and had watched a man drown. She had never swum before, never entered the water at all, and yet she had known she could. She watched horrified as the boat went over.

"White squall!" Gar shouted up the stairs. And indeed the entire world had turned white, as white and as impenetrable as a thick fog. The surface of the sea was foaming, and the wild wind scraped off the curling crests of waves and flung the spume into the air.

May raced down the stairs. "Where you going, May?" But she did not bother to answer. "May, don't be a fool. That wind will scrape you right off the island!"

"What's that fool girl doing?" Hepzibah said as Gar came back in the house. "She flew out of here like a bat out of hell."

"Shut your mouth, you old witch!" Gar seethed.

Zeeba sank back in her rocker, her eyes wide with disbelief.

But May was racing down the path. Her father stood in the doorway. Within seconds her figure disappeared into the thick white.

"YOU ARE THE WORLD!"

MAY MOVED THROUGH THE WATER as she had never moved before. It was odd that not that far from the surface it was calm, a different world. She sliced across the seafloor to where she thought the sailboat had tipped. She soon saw its spars upside down in the water. It must have capsized completely, but where was Hugh? Then she saw him a few yards from the boat. He was trying to swim back to it to hang on. She surfaced to get some air and caught sight of a surfboat! They had launched one from the rescue service and it was closing in on Hugh. But then to her horror as it drew closer she saw only one oarsman, and that oarsman had shipped his paddle and was standing up on the bow of the boat with Lucky! Rudd!

He raised the harpoon and was about to launch it directly at Hugh's chest as he swam—swam toward the surfboat. Swam toward his own executioner. The next few seconds were a blur for May. She only remembered jetting high out of the water, plunging back in just beneath where Hugh swam, and the next thing she knew she had him. The harpoon cut through the water, barely missing them both. She surfaced briefly. Hugh's eyes were closed. But he was still breathing.

The swirling whiteness of the squall had cleared. The wind abated, but there was Rudd, still in the boat, with yet a new harpoon in his hand. He was scanning the surface, looking slightly bewildered. May had her arms over Hugh's chest. She was gripping him from behind and his head obscured hers. It only took Rudd an instant to spot him. He set down the harpoon and began rowing again toward them. The wind was behind him and he was making good time. There was only one choice left for May. She had to take Hugh under. She took an immense breath of air, then pressing her mouth against his, she dove deep. She felt the air stream out of her at a slow, steady pace, then inhaled some back from his mouth into hers. She had to be his lungs as long as they traveled together beneath the surface, out of sight of Rudd. *Breathe, breathe, Hugh. Breathe.*

She swam as fast as she could, as long as she could. She swam toward The Bones. When she surfaced a fog had swept in, a blessed fog. Rudd could not find them. It was as thick and as dense as the whiteness of the squall. *Please, God*, she prayed. *Let the fog last. Let it last!*

She dragged Hugh up onto the ledge, which at this tide was almost entirely out of the water. His eyes were still closed. He appeared unconscious, but he was breathing. There was a bruise forming on his right cheek, but she had still never seen a lovelier face. She traced the spot where those deep wonderful creases appeared every time he laughed. How she loved his face when he laughed. He had begun to stir; she saw his eyes moving behind the pale blue veins in his lids. Suddenly she was looking into the soft gray light of his gaze.

"May?"

"Yes, you'll be fine, Hugh. But he tried to kill you. He'll try again."

"But, May, you saved me."

"Why were you such a fool to go out in this weather?"

"Love, I told you—it knows no season."

She looked away from him and began to cry. Through the fog, the scales of her tail sparkled.

"May, why are you crying?"

"You know what I am now."

He sat up slowly. He was looking at her tail. She could feel his eyes on it even though she would not turn her head to look at his face.

"And what are you?"

"You can see." She stirred the flukes of her tail in the lapping water. "I am less than human."

He gazed at the tail as it stirred the water. She looked at his eyes as they swept from the flukes to the hem of where her dress lay wet across what would have been her knees on dry land. He turned his head and smiled at her so sweetly she thought her heart might break.

"And if you are less than human, what does that make Rudd? We should all be so human as you, May."

A sob convulsed her. Hugh took her in his arms.

"Look at me, May. Look at me."

"I can't. I can't. I am ashamed."

"No! No, never! What are you ashamed of? These lovely scales that make the fog so bright? The brightness of your mind? I love you for all these things, May. You are the stars. You are a galaxy unbound and come to earth. You are what makes the invisible world visible. I love you. You are the world to me!"

May pressed her head against Hugh's chest. The thud of his human heart seemed to blend with the sound of the waves splashing against the rocks. She sighed. For the moment, nothing existed but the two of them. There was no Rudd. No Zeeba. They were two stars burning in a secluded patch of night sky.